George M. Fenn

Eli's Children

The chronicles of an unhappy family - Vol. 3

George M. Fenn

Eli's Children
The chronicles of an unhappy family - Vol. 3

ISBN/EAN: 9783337406486

Printed in Europe, USA, Canada, Australia, Japan

Cover: Foto ©Andreas Hilbeck / pixelio.de

More available books at **www.hansebooks.com**

ELI'S CHILDREN.

The Chronicles of an Unhappy Family.

BY

GEORGE MANVILLE FENN,

AUTHOR OF

"THE VICAR'S PEOPLE;" "THE PARSON O' DUMFORD," ET

IN THREE VOLUMES.

VOLUME III.

LONDON:

CHAPMAN & HALL, LIMITED, 11. HENRIETTA ST., W.C.

1882.

Bungay:
CLAY AND TAYLOR, PRINTERS.

CONTENTS OF VOLUME III.

Book II.—(*Continued.*)

 CONTENTS.

Book III.—The Barrister's Day.

CHAPTER I.

CHAPTER II.

CHAPTER III.

CHAPTER IV.

CHAPTER V.

CHAPTER VI.

CHAPTER VII.

CHAPTER VIII.

CHAPTER IX.

CHAPTER X.

CHAPTER XI.

CHAPTER XII.

CHAPTER XIII.

CHAPTER XIV.

CHAPTER XV.

CHAPTER XVI.

ELI'S CHILDREN.

BOOK II.—(*CONTINUED.*)

CHAPTER V.

WHAT PLAN NEXT?

JAMES MAGNUS had just struggled to his knees, feeling half mad with rage at his impotence, for it was only now that he fully realized how terribly he had been reduced by his illness. Here before him was the man whom he had to thank for his sufferings, and against whom for other reasons as well he nourished a bitter hatred; and yet, instead of being able to seize him by the throat and force the scoundrel to his knees, he was as helpless as a child.

"Dog! villain!" he panted, as he staggered up, and made at the fellow; but Jock Morrison gave him a contemptuous look for answer, and turned to him, but seemed to alter his mind, and as if alarmed at what he had done, started off at a brisk trot; while after vainly looking round for help, Magnus tottered towards the edge of the cliff, his eyes starting and the great drops of perspiration gathering upon his face.

For a few moments he dared not approach the extreme verge, for everything seemed to be swimming before his eyes, but at last, horror-stricken, and trembling in every limb, he went down on hands and knees, crept to the spot where Artingale had gone over, and peered down, expecting to see the mangled remains of his poor friend lying upon the stones beneath.

"Ahoy!" came from below, in the well-known voice of Artingale; and then, as Magnus saw his friend some twenty feet below, trying to clamber back, he uttered a low sigh, and sank back fainting upon the turf.

For in spite of Jock Morrison's murderous

intent, fate had been kind to Harry Artingale, who had been hurled over the edge in one of the few places where instead of going down perpendicularly, the friable cliff was broken up into ledges and slopes, upon one of which the young man had fallen and clung for his life to the rugged pieces of stone, slipping in a little avalanche of fragments some twenty or thirty feet farther than his first fall of about ten. Here he managed to check himself, while one of the largest fragments of stone that he had started in his course went on, and as he clung there he saw it leap, as it were, from beside him, and a few seconds after there came up a dull crash from where the stone had struck and splintered, two hundred feet below.

" I shall lose my nerve," he thought, " if I stop here ;" and rousing himself into action, he began to climb back, and was making his way up the steep slope without much difficulty, when he saw his friend's ghastly face for a moment, peering over the edge, and then it disappeared.

" Poor old fellow, it has made him giddy," muttered Artingale, as he drew himself up higher and higher, clinging close to the face of the slope and placing his feet cautiously till he found himself with his hands resting upon a ledge only a few feet below the top of the cliff.

If he could only get upon this ledge the rest would be easy, but unless he could draw himself up by the strength of his muscles, he felt that he must wait for help, and the task was one of no little difficulty, for there was no firm hold for his hands.

He knew that if he waited for help he must lose his nerve by thinking of his perilous position, while if he tried to draw himself up and did not succeed in reaching the ledge he felt that he must fall.

He dared not pause to think of the consequences of that fall, for though he had escaped so far, it was not likely that he would be so fortunate again.

He was standing now with his feet on a piece of crumbling sandstone, which was likely enough to give way if he tried to make a spring upwards.

Still, there was nothing else to be done, and

drawing in a deep breath, he remained perfectly motionless before making the supreme effort.

His hands were only a few inches above his head, and he began searching about with them now for a crevice into which he could thrust his fingers, but the blind search was vain, and feeling that this was hopeless, he let his eyes fall to scan the surface of the rock below his chest for some fresh foothold; but there was none, unless he cut a niche in the soft sandstone, and he had no knife. If he climbed to the right he would be in no better position; if to the left, he would be in a worse; so once more drawing a long breath, he began cautiously to draw himself up higher and higher by sheer force of muscle, till his eyes were level with the edge of the shelf; then an inch or two higher, and then he felt that his hands were giving way—that he was falling—that all was over, and that he must be dashed to pieces, when, in his agony, he saw an opening, a mere crack across the shelf, but it was sufficient for him to force in the fingers of one hand with a desperate effort, and then, how he knew not, he placed the other beside it.

He could cling here and force feet and knees against the face of the rock, and in the struggle of the next few moments he raised himself higher, scrambled on to the ledge, rose panting and with every nerve in his body quivering, seized hold of a stone above him, thrust his feet into a niche or two, gained the top of the cliff, and, unable to keep up the tension longer, he loosed the strain upon his nerves and sank down beside his friend, trembling in every limb.

This, however, did not last many moments, for, shaking off the feeling of his own horror, Artingale rose, drew down and buttoned his wristbands, looking pityingly the while at his friend, and then caught up his coat and threw it on.

The next moment he was kneeling beside Magnus, who soon after opened his eyes.

"Ah, Harry," he said, feebly, "you didn't know what a miserable reed you had for a friend."

"Nonsense, man! How are you? Did the blackguard hurt you?"

"No, scarcely at all. I'm weak as a rat. But you!"

"Oh, I'm all right. Only a little skin off my elbows and varnish off my toes. Which way did the brute go?"

"Over the hill yonder," said Magnus.

"Where he may go," said Artingale, "for hang me if I go after him to-day. Why, confound him, he's as strong as a bull. I couldn't have thought a man could be so powerful. But let's get back, old fellow. Can you walk?"

"Oh yes, I'm better now," said Magnus feebly; "but I shall never forgive myself for failing you at such a pinch."

"Never mind the failing, Jemmy: but pinch it was; the blackguard nearly broke my ribs. One moment: let me look down."

He walked to the edge and looked over the cliff, realizing more plainly now the terrible risk he had run, for his escape had been narrow indeed, and in spite of his attempt to preserve his composure, he could not help feeling a peculiar moisture gathering in the palms of his hands. But he laughed it off as he took Magnus's arm, and drew it through his own, saying,

"It's a great blessing, my dear boy, that I took off this coat. It would have been completely spoiled."

"You had an awfully narrow escape."

"Yes; and it is almost a pity the brute did not kill me," said Artingale, coolly.

"Harry!"

"Well, if he had, the police would have hunted the scoundrel down, then he would have been hung, and little Julie could have rested in peace."

"And Cynthia?" said Magnus, with a sad smile.

"Ah, yes! poor little darling, she would have broken her heart. But I say, old fellow, it's a pity the scoundrel got away. What are we to do?"

"He must be taken," exclaimed Magnus, "at any cost. It was a murderous attempt on your life."

"Humph! yes, but he might swear that I tried to throw him over first. It was a fight, old fellow, and I got the worst of it."

" But he must be taken."

" No," said Artingale, " I think not, old fellow ; his is a peculiar case, and we can't be going into witness-boxes and answering all sorts of questions. After to day's adventure down below on the beach, I don't see that we can move. No, Magnus, there are things that must be hushed up, and this is one of them. But we must do something. I declare I'll mount a revolver, and have a shot at the brute if he annoys them again, legal or illegal."

" Impossible," said Magnus, bitterly.

" By Jove ; if he'd only go down home again and get up to some of his poaching tricks. I tell you what, Magnus, old man," he said. setting his teeth, " I hope fate will never place me with my men down at Gatley, going to meet a poaching party led by Jock Morrison. If she does—well——"

" Well what ? "

" I hope I sha'n't have a gun in my hand."

" You must persuade Mr. Mallow to leave here."

" What ! just as he has come down for

Julia's health. No, my dear fellow, you might just as well try to move a rock. But I say, our first attempt at playing detectives don't seem to have been much of a success."

" No," said Magnus, dreamily. " Let's get back."

" What are you thinking about, old man," said Artingale, after a pause.

" I was thinking whether the fellow could be bribed to go away."

" Oh, yes, easily," said Artingale, " and he'd go and come back next week, and levy blackmail wherever the family went, while the very fact of his having been paid off would give the affair an ugly look if ever we had occasion to drag the scoundrel before the judge."

" Then what is to be done ? " said Magnus, angrily, " the police must be consulted."

" No : won't do," said Artingale, decisively. " Wait a bit, Jemmy, and I'll hit upon some plan. Unfortunately, we live in these degraded times when that fine old institution the press-gang is no more."

" This is no time for levity, Harry," said Magnus, bitterly.

"Levity! My dear boy, my feelings towards that fellow are full of anything but levity. He nearly killed me, and that is no joke; and—oh! horror of horror! I did not expect this—here's Perry-Morton."

He was quite right, for the idol of the early masters' clique was advancing to meet them after failing to see poor Julia, who with throbbing pulses and cheeks now pale, now burning with fever, was sobbing in her sister's arms.

CHAPTER VI.

UNSELFISH PROCEEDINGS.

"Frightened away? Not a doubt about it," said Artingale. "I feel as if I had been a martyr, and offered myself up as a sacrifice."

"Martyr—sacrifice!" cried Cynthia, looking at the speaker keenly, and with her bright little face flushing. "Now, Harry, I'll never forgive you. I'm sure you've been keeping something back. There, see how guilty you look! Oh, shame! shame!"

Artingale protested that he had been silent only from the best motives, was accused of deceit and want of confidence, and ended by making a full confession of the whole incident, after which he had to take Cynthia and show her the exact spot before his shuddering little companion condescended to forgive.

"And when was this, sir?"

"This day month," said Artingale, humbly, "and we have not seen him since. Magnus and I have watched, and searched, and hunted, and done everything possible; but, as I say, I think I have been the sacrifice. He believes he killed me, and is afraid to show."

"Perhaps he has committed suicide out of remorse," said Cynthia.

"Just the sort of fellow who would," replied Artingale, with a dry look.

"Now you are laughing at me," cried Cynthia, pettishly. "I declare, Harry, I believe you are tired of me, and want to quarrel. I've been too easy with you, sir, and ought to have kept you at a distance."

More protesting and pardoning took place here, all very nice in their way, but of no interest to any save the parties concerned.

"You must get Julie to come out more now," said Artingale. "Tell her there is nothing to mind."

"I can't make poor Julie out at all," said

Cynthia thoughtfully. "She seems so strange and quiet. That man must have frightened her dreadfully."

"Did she tell you about it?"

"Very little, and if I press her she shudders, and seems ready to burst out sobbing. Then I have to comfort her by telling her that I am sure she will never see him any more, and when I say this she looks at me so strangely."

"What does mamma say?"

"Oh, only that Julie is foolish and hysterical. She doesn't understand her at all. Poor mamma never did understand us girls, I'm sure," said Cynthia, with a profound look of wisdom upon her little face.

"And papa?"

"Oh, poor dear papa thinks of nothing but seeing us married and— Oh, Harry, I *am* ashamed."

"What of?" he cried, catching her in his arms and kissing her tenderly. "Why, Cynthy, I never knew before what a fine old fellow the pater is. He is up to par in my estimation now."

"Is that meant for a joke, sir?" said Cynthia mockingly.

"Joke?—joke? I don't know what you mean."

"Never mind now; but you need not be so pleased about what papa says. I think it's very cruel—wanting to get rid of us."

"I don't," exclaimed Artingale, laughing.

"Then you want to see poor Julie married to that dreadful Perry-Morton?"

"No, I don't; I want her to have dear old James Magnus. I say, Cynthy. We won't be selfish, eh? We won't think about ourselves, will we? Let's try and make other people happy."

"Yes, Harry, we will."

It was wonderful to see the sincerity with which these two young people spoke, and how eagerly they set to making plans for other people's happiness—a process which seemed to need a great deal of clinging together for mutual support, twining about of arms, and looking long and deeply into each other's eyes for counsel. Then Artingale's hair was a little too much over his forehead for the thoughts of Cynthia to flow freely, and it had to be smoothed back by a little white hand with busy fingers. But that hair was obstinate, and it was not until the little pinky fingers had several times been moistened between Cynthia's ruddy lips and drawn over the objecting strands of hair that they could be forced to retain the desired position.

After the performance of such a kindly service Artingale would have been ungrateful if he had not thanked her in the most affectionate way his brain could suggest, a proceeding of which, with all due modesty, the young lady seemed highly to approve.

Then Harry's tie was not quite right, and the new collar stud had to be admired, and a great deal more of this very unselfish *eau sucrée* had to be imbibed before Julia again came on the *tapis*, her entrance being heralded by a sister's sigh.

" Poor Julie ! " said Cynthia.

" Oh, yes; poor Julia. Now, look here, pet, I dare say it's very shocking, and if it were known the Rector would be sure to give me my *congé*."

"Oh, I would never think of telling him. Harry."

"That's right. Well, as I was saying. if she marries Perry-Morton she will be miserable."

"Horribly," assented Cynthia.

"And if she marries old Magnus she will be very happy."

"But are you sure that Mr. Magnus really loves her ?"

"He worships her. I'm sure of it."

"Then it would be wicked, wouldn't it. Harry, to keep them apart ?"

"I should think it as bad as murder to keep us apart."

"Should you, Harry ?"

"Yes." And more unselfish proceedings.

"Then, as papa and mamma have made a mistake, don't you think we ought to help them ?"

"Yes," said Artingale, "but how ? Magnus hangs back. He says he is sure that Julia does not think of him in the slightest degree. What do you say ?"

"I don't know what to say." cried Cynthia

thoughtfully, "only that I am sure she hates Perry-Morton. She says she does."

" But does she show any liking for Magnus ? "

" N—no, I'm afraid not. But does that matter, dear ? "

" Well, I should think not," replied Artingale thoughtfully. " Magnus loves her very much, and I'm sure no girl could help loving him in return. I almost feel jealous when he talks to you."

" No, you don't, Harry," retorted Cynthia, recommencing operations upon the obstinate lock of hair.

" Then what is to be done ? " said Artingale, at last, after another long display of unselfishness.

" I'm sure I don't know, Harry. It almost seems as if Julia was ready to let herself go with the stream. She is so quiet and strange and reserved. I don't know what to make of her. She keeps fancying she sees that man."

" But she don't see him."

" Oh no: it is impossible ; but she is so

changed. I find her sometimes sitting and thinking, looking straight before her as if she were in a dream. Bring Mr. Magnus here more often."

"Here?"

"Well, no; to Lawford. I'll coax papa into asking him. Oh, I say, what a capital idea!" cried Cynthia, clapping her hands. "I have it. Her portrait!"

"Her portrait!" exclaimed Artingale. starting, as he recalled the scene in his friend's studio.

"Yes; the very thing. You take him down to Gatley, and papa shall ask Mr. Magnus over to Lawford to paint Julia's portrait, and then there will be such long sittings, Harry; and Mr. Magnus will have to look at her so patiently. and move this hand there and that hand here, and get her into quite the correct pose. Oh, Harry. what fun!"

"Why, you cunning little witch," he exclaimed; "if Magnus does not jump at the idea. he deserves to lose her."

Then there came a little more unselfishness

and a little disinterested proceeding, which was interrupted by the entrance of Julia herself, looking very pale and sad. There was a far-off, distant aspect about her eyes, as of one who was thinking deeply of some great trouble, but she smiled affectionately when Cynthia spoke, after which the conspirators exchanged glances, and Artingale went away.

CHAPTER VII.

THEY were to be busy times at the Rectory that winter, for the servants left in charge heard that there was to be a great deal of company.

The Gatley domestics too had to make preparations, for Lord Artingale intended to entertain that season. A room was set apart for Mr. Magnus the great artist. Miss Mallow's brothers were expected to come over from the Rectory to shoot, and Mr. Cyril Mallow, it was anticipated, would be asked to bring his young wife and stay there at the fine old house—a fact, for Sage was a member now of the Mallow family, and Harry Artingale liked her as much as he disliked her husband.

There was plenty of gossip rife in Lawford, and on the strength of old Michael Ross saying, when he was told that Mr. Magnus the painter was coming down, that his son Luke knew him, having met him at a London club, the report ran through the place that Luke Ross was getting to be quite a big man, and had become a friend of Lord Artingale.

"Not that that's much," said Fullerton, at the King's Head, "for the young lord isn't what his father was. Old Lord Artingale wouldn't have married one of Mallow's girls, I know, nor yet made boon companions of those two sons and Luke Ross."

"I don't think you need put them all together," said Tomlinson, with a sly laugh; "Luke Ross wouldn't be very good friends with the man who stole his lass. If he would he's not the Luke Ross that he was when he was down here."

In due time the blinds went up at Gatley and at the Rectory, and the tradespeople who had been ready to discuss the shortcomings of the Rector were obsequious enough in soliciting his orders now the family had returned.

They had made a long stay at Hastings, for the Rector fancied it did Mrs. Mallow good. She seemed to smile more, and to look brighter, he told himself, and he would stand and beam at her as he wheeled her couch to the open window when it was fine, and watch her gazing at the sea with the greatest of satisfaction.

Frank had made journeys to and from London, making at the latter place Cyril's house at Kensington his head-quarters, and frequently being his companion away from home.

Julia was no better, in spite of the opinion of the doctor, who said that she had decidedly gained tone, and that the change now to her native air would complete the cure; so the family returned to Lawford as the winter drew near, and, as a matter of course, Lord Artingale soon found his way back to Gatley.

There was some preparation too at Kilby, for Portlock said that it was his turn to have the young folks to stay.

"They may go to the rectory as much as they like, mother,"—a title he invariably gave Mrs. Portlock, on the *lucus a non lucendo* principle,—"but I mean to have them stay here; not that I'm particularly fond of Master Cyril; but there, he's the little lassie's husband, and it's all right."

"But you asked John Berry and Rue to come and bring the little ones," said Mrs. Portlock.

"Well, I know that, old lady. Isn't Kilby big enough to hold the lot? Let's have the place made a bit cheerful; I like to hear a good hearty shout of laughter now and then, and you've taken to do nothing else lately but grumble softly and scold."

"It's a wicked story, Joseph, and you know it," cried Mrs. Portlock, as the Churchwarden turned away from her and winked at the cat; "and as for noise, I'm sure you make enough in the house without wanting more."

"Never mind, let's have more; and Cyril Mallow can shoot down the rabbits, for they're rather getting ahead."

As he spoke he had been filling his pipe,

and he now took out a letter, read it, and slowly folded it up for a pipe-light, saying to himself—

"He's no business to want me to lend him a hundred pound after what I so lately did for them as a start."

James Magnus had been invited to take Julia's portrait, the Rector, artfully prompted thereto by Cynthia, accompanying the commission by a very warm invitation to stay at the rectory as much as he could while the portrait was in progress, as he heard that Mr. Magnus was coming down to Gatley.

Artingale dropped in at his friend's studio on the very day that he received the Rector's letter—of course by accident, based upon a hint from Cynthia; and found Magnus sitting thoughtfully by his easel, pretending to paint, but doing nothing.

"Why, Mag, you look well enough and strong enough now to thrash Hercules himself, in the person of our gipsy friend."

"Yes, I feel myself again," was the reply. "By the way, Harry, I've had an invitation to Lawford."

"Indeed! I'm very glad. I go down to-morrow."

"The Rector wishes me to paint his daughter's portrait."

"Not Cynthia's?"

"No, that of his daughter Julia."

"Why, Magnus," said Artingale, smiling to himself and laying his hand upon his friend's arm, "could you wish for a greater pleasure?"

Magnus looked at him so fixedly for a few moments that Artingale felt that he must be suspected; but it was not so, the artist only shook his head, and there was a bitter look in his face, as he spoke again.

"Pleasure!" he said; "how can it be a pleasure to me? Harry, my boy, how can you be so thoughtless. Do you think I could be guilty of so dishonourable an act?"

"Dishonourable?"

"Yes," cried Magnus passionately. "Should I not go there on false pretences to try and win that poor girl from the man to whom she is engaged?"

"But, my dear fellow, it is a folly of her father's invention; she detests this Perry-

Morton, as every right-thinking, matter-of-fact girl would. Why, the fellow dances attendance upon every woman of fashion, and deserves to be encountered with any weapon one could seize Tell me, do you think it right that she should marry such a man?"

"No: certainly not. No more right than that she should be deluded into marrying another man she did not love."

"But she would love you, Mag. My dear fellow, don't refuse to go. Accept the offer for Julia's sake—for Cynthia's and mine. if you like. Don't be scrupulous about trifles. I tell you she is a dear, sweet girl, and I know your secret. She is heart-whole now, but if she began to learn that there was some one who really loved her, she would fly to him like a young bird does to her mate."

"Very pretty sophistry, Harry Artingale. When you have had your fling of life I should advise you to turn Jesuit."

"Don't talk stuff, my dear fellow. Take my advice. Go down with me at once to Gatley, and make your hay while the sun shines. I guarantee the result."

"What, that I shall be kicked out as a scoundrel?"

"Nonsense! kicked out, indeed! That you will win little Julia's heart."

"As I should deserve to be," continued Magnus, without heeding his friend's words. "No, Harry, I am not blind. I can read Julia Mallow's heart better, perhaps, than I can read my own, and I know that, whoever wins her love, I shall not be the man. As to her marriage with this wretched butterfly of the day, I can say nothing—do nothing. That rests with the family."

"James Magnus," cried Artingale, angrily, "sophistry or no, I wouldn't stand by and see the woman I loved taken from before my eyes by that contemptible cad. The world might say what it liked about honour and dishonour, and perhaps it might blame you, while, at the same time, it will praise up and deliver eulogies upon the wedding of that poor girl to Perry-Morton. But what is the opinion of such a world as that worth? Come, come—take your opportunity, and win and wear her. Hang it all, Jemmy!

don't say the young Lochinvar was in the wrong."

"You foolish, enthusiastic boy," said Magnus, smiling, "so you think I study the sayings or doings of the fragment of our people that you call the world? No, I look elsewhere for the judgment, and, may be, most of all in my own heart. There, say no more about it. I have made up my mind."

"And I have made up mine," cried Artingale, sharply, "that you have not the spirit of a man."

He left the studio hot and angry, went straight to his chambers, and soon after he was on his way to Gatley, having determined to see Cynthia at once for a fresh unselfish discussion upon Julia's state.

CHAPTER VIII.

A VISIT FROM BROTHER JOCK.

"WELL," said Smithson, the tailor, as he looked up from a square patch that he was inserting in the seat of a fellow-townsman's trousers, "the parson has his faults, and as a family I don't like 'em, but when they're down it do make a difference to the town."

This was as the cobble stones of the little place rattled to the beating of horses' hoofs, while a bright-looking little equestrian party passed along the main street; Cynthia mounted on a favourite mare belonging to Lord Artingale, one which she was always pleading to ride, and one whereon her slave loved to see her, though he always sent her over to the rectory in fear and trembling, ordering the groom who took her to give her a good gallop on the way to tame her down.

Not that there was the slightest disposition to vice in the beautiful little creature, she was only spirited, or, as the people in his lordship's stable said, "a bit larky," and when Cynthia was mounted there was plenty of excuse for the young man's pride.

"I shall never have patience to ride an old plodding, humble-stumble horse again, Harry," the little maiden used to say. "It's like sitting on air; and she is such a dear, and it's a shame to put two such great bits in her mouth."

"It is only so that you might check her easily, Cynthy," said Artingale, anxiously. "You need not mind; with such a hand as yours at the rein they don't hurt her mouth."

"But I'm sure they do, Harry," cried Cynthia; "and look how she champs them up, and what a foam she makes, and when she snorts and throws up her head it flies over my new riding-habit."

"Never mind, my beautiful little darling," he whispered; "you shall have a new riding-

habit every week if you like, only you must
have the big curb for Mad Sal. Oh, I'd give
something if Magnus could reproduce you now
with one instantaneous touch of his brush,
and——"

"Hush! you silly boy," she whispered
reprovingly, as the mare ambled on. "This is
not the time and place to talk such nonsense."

Nonsense or no, it produced a very satis-
factory glow in the little maiden's heart—a
glow which shone in her soft cheeks, and
made her eyes flash as they rode on.

These riding parties were very frequent,
Cyril and Frank joining; sometimes John
Magnus, but never upon the days when Julia
was prevailed upon to mount.

For Cyril was supposed to be staying with
his young wife at the farm, but he passed the
greater part of his time at the rectory, when
he was not at Gatley with his brother.

It was a pleasant time, for the roads were
hard that winter, the air crisp and dry, giving
a tone to the nerves and muscles, and an
elasticity to the mind, that made even quiet
James Magnus look more like himself, while

there were times when Julia looked less dreamy
and pale, and as if the thoughts of her
persecutor were less frequent in her breast.

Sage and she had grown more intimate, as
if there were feelings in common between
them, the quiet toleration of Cyril's wife
ripening fast into affection, so that, as
Cynthia's time was so much taken up by Lord
Artingale, Julia and Sage were a good deal
together, the latter being her sister-in-law's
companion in her visiting rounds, when, to the
Rev. Lawrence Paulby's satisfaction, she tried
to counteract some of the prevalent ill-feeling
against the Mallow family by calls here and
there amongst the parishioners.

One place where they often called was at
the ford of the river, to have a chat with little
Mrs. Morrison, where somehow there seemed
to be quite a magnetic attraction; Cyril's wife
sitting down in the neatly-kept little place to
gaze almost in silence at the wheelwright's
pretty young wife, while, as if drawn there
against her will, Julia would stop and talk.

The river was very pretty just there even in
winter, brawling and babbling over the gravel

before settling down calm and still as it flowed slowly amongst the deep holes beneath the willow pollards, where the big fish were known to lie. And more than once sister and sister-in-law came upon Cyril in one or other of the fields, trying after the big jack that no one yet had caught.

"I know he's about here somewhere," said Cyril, over and over again. "He lies in wait for the dace that come off the shallows, and I mean to have him before I've done."

That was an artful jack though, for it must have understood Cyril Mallow and his wiles, obstinately refusing to be caught.

Julia used to look very serious when she saw him there again and again, but she felt afraid to speak, for the confidence that had existed between her and her old maid seemed to have passed away, and when their eyes met at times there was a curious shrinking look on either side; and so the time went on.

One day Tom Morrison was busily at work at a piece of well-seasoned ash with his spoke-shave. The day was bright and keen and cold, but he was stripped to shirt and trousers, the neck unfastened, sleeves rolled up, and a look of calm satisfaction in his face as his muscles tightened and he drew off the thin spiral shavings from the piece of wood.

In old days the workshop used to resound with snatches of song, or his rather melodious whistling; but of late, since the loss of his little one, he had grown cold and grave, working in a quiet, subdued manner; and those who knew him said that he was nursing up his revenge against the parson.

Fullerton gave him several jobs that should by rights have gone to Biggins the carpenter, and he once went so far as to say—

"They tell me you never go to church now, Tom Morrison."

"Would you like it painted stone-colour or white, Mr. Fullerton?" said Tom Morrison, quietly.

"Oh—er—white," replied Fullerton, and he said no more upon that occasion.

It was about a month later, over another job, that Fullerton ventured another advance, and this time he said, as he was leaving the workshop, and holding out his hand—

"Good-bye, Morrison. Oh, by the way, we've got Samuel Mumbey, D.D., at the chapel on Sunday. Preaches twice. We'll find you good seats if you and Mrs. Morrison will come. Ours is a nice woshup, Morrison, a very nice woshup, as you would say if you was to try."

"Thankye, sir," said Tom Morrison, stolidly, and again Fullerton said no more till he was some distance away, when he rubbed his hands softly and smiled a satisfied smile, saying to himself—

"I should like to save Tom Morrison and his wife from the pit."

Tom Morrison was hard at work, thinking sometimes of his pretty little wife in the cottage, and how thin and careworn she had grown of late. He wondered whether it was his fault, and because he had been so hard and cold since he had lost his little child and quarrelled with the Rector; whether, too, he ought not to try and bring back some of the brightness to her face, when it seemed as if so much light as usual did not shine in upon his work.

He raised his head, and found that there were a pair of thick arms leaning on the window-sill, and a great bearded face resting upon them, the owner's eyes staring hard at him.

"Hallo, Jock!" he said, quietly.

"What, Tommy!" was the deep-toned reply; and then there was a pause, as Tom Morrison felt angry as he thought of his brother's ne'er-do-well life, and then of his having been hard and cold of late, and this seemed the time for beginning in another line.

"Long time since I've seen you, Jock," he said, quietly.

"Aye, 'tis, Tommy. Working hard as usual."

"Aye, working hard, Jock," said Tom, resting his spoke-shave. "Thou used to be a good workman, Jock. Why not take to it again?"

"Me? Work? Wheer?

"I'll give you plenty to do, Jock, and find wage for it, lad, if thou'lt drop being a shack and sattle down."

Jock Morrison laughed in a deep and silent manner.

"Nay, lad, nay," he said at last. "Thankye

kindly, Tom, all the same. What's the good
o' working ? "

" To be respectable and save money."

" I don't want to be respectable. I don't
want to save money, lad. There's plenty do
that wi'out me."

" But how will it be when thou grows old
and sick, lad ? "

" Why then, Tommy, I shall die ; just the
same as you will. I'm happy my way, lad.
Thou'rt happy thy way. Folk say I'm a shack,
and a blackguard, and a poacher. Well, let
'em ; I don't keer."

" Nay, don't say that, lad," said Tom
Morrison ; " I don't like it. I'd like to see
thee tak' to work and be a man."

" Ha, ha, ha, Tom ! Why, I'm a bigger and
a stronger man than thou art anyways. Nay,
I don't keer for work. Let them do it as likes.
I don't want boxing up in a house or a shed. I
want to be in the free air, and to come and go
as I like. I see no good in your ways. Let
me bide."

Tom looked at him in a dull, careworn way.

" Why, look ye here, lad," cried Jock.

"Here am I as blithe and hearty as a bird, and here are you, plod, plod, plod, from day to day, round and round, like old Michael Ross's blind horse in the bark mill. I look as hearty as a buck; you look ten years older, and as if life warn't worth a gill o' ale."

"I wean't argue with you, Jock," said Tom, quietly. "You must go your own gate, I suppose, and I'll go mine."

"Aye, that's it, Tommy."

"But if ever you like to try being an honest man again, lad, I'm thy own brother, and I'll give thee a lift best way I can for the old folks' sake."

Jock Morrison left the window, and came like a modern edition of Astur of the stately stride round to the door, walked in amongst the shavings and sawdust, gave his brother a tremendous slap on the back, and then seized his hand and stood shaking it for a good minute by the old Dutch clock in the corner.

He did not speak, but half sat down afterwards upon the bench, watching his brother as Tom resumed his work.

"How's little wife?" said Jock at last.

"Not hearty, Jock," said Tom Morrison. "She's pined a deal lately. Never got over losing the bairn."

There was a spell of silence here, and then Tom said quietly—

"Go in and have a crust o' bread and cheese, Jock, and a mug of ale. The little lass has been baking this morning."

"Aye, I will," said Jock, and thrusting his hands down into his pockets, he rolled like a great ship on a heaving sea out of the workshop, along the road, and then through the little garden, and without ceremony into the cottage, stooping his head as he passed in at the low door.

CHAPTER IX.

A CRUEL CHARGE.

POLLY was busy at needle-work, and as the great fellow strode in and stood staring at her, she started up and seemed as if about to run away.

"You here, Jock, again?" she faltered.

"Aye! here I am again," he said, in a deep growl, as he fixed her with his eye, while she trembled before him and his fierce look.

"I'm glad—to see you, Jock," she said, faintly, and she glanced towards the door.

"That's a lie," he growled, and then he laughed grimly, but only for his face to darken into a savage scowl. "Tom said I was to come in, lass."

"Oh, you've seen Tom!" she said, as if relieved.

"Aye, and he said I was to have some bread and cheese and beer."

"Yes, Jock," she cried; "I'll get it out."

She had to pass him, and he caught her hand in his, towering over her and making her shiver, as if fascinated by his gaze, as Julia Mallow had been a score of times.

"Stop!" he said, in a low, deep voice. "Wait a bit. I don't want the bread and cheese. Look here, Polly."

"Yes, Jock, yes," she panted; "but don't hurt me."

"Hurt ye!" he growled; "I feel as if I could kill thee."

"Jock!"

"Look here, Polly. I came to see Tom to-day to jump upon him, and call him a fool, and give him back what he's given me for not sattling down and marrying and being respectable. I was going to laugh at him, and show him what his respectable married life was."

"I—I don't understand you, Jock," she said, faintly.

"It's 'a lie," he growled. "I was going to laugh at him, but, damn it, he's so good a chap I hadn't the heart to mak' him miserable any more than he is about that poor bairn he thinks was his, and I——"

"How dare you!" cried Polly, flaming up, and trying to tear away her hand; but he held it fast, and, in spite of her indignation, she cowered before his fierce, almost savage looks.

"How dare I?" he growled. "Didn't young Serrol run after you at the house when you were at Mallow's? Hasn't he been after you ever since? Isn't he every day nearly hanging about the river there fishing, so as to come and talk to thee? Curse you!" he growled. "This is a wife, is it? But, by G—d, it shan't go on, for I'll take him by the neck next time he's fishing yonder by the willow stumps, and I'll howd him under-water and drownd him as I would a pup."

"Oh, Jock, Jock, Jock," she cried, sinking on her knees.

"I will—I will, by G—d!" he cried, in

a fierce growl; "and then you may go and
say I did it, when they find his cursed carcase,
and get me hung for drownding thy lover."

"It's a lie!" cried Polly, springing up
and speaking passionately. "Cyril Mallow is
no lover of mine. I hate and detest him,
but never dared tell poor Tom how he came
and troubled me. But I'll tell him now; I'll
confess all to him. I'd sooner he killed me
than you should insult me with such lies."

She made a rush for the door, and had
reached it, but, with an activity not to be
expected in his huge frame, Jock swept round
one great arm, seized her, and drew her back,
quivering with indignation.

"Let me go," she cried, passionately.
"Tom! Tom!"

"Howd thy noise," he growled, and once
more she shrunk cowering from his fierce eyes.
"Now then, say that again. S'elp your G—d,
Serrol Mallow is nothing to thee, and never
has been."

"I won't," she cried, passionately, and
she flashed up once more and met his gaze.
"How dare you ask me such a thing?"

"Say it, lass—say it out honest, lass—is what I say true?"

"No," she cried, gazing full in his eyes. "It's a cruel, cruel lie. Let me go. I'll tell Tom now—every word—everything that man has said, and——"

Jock let his great hand sink from Polly's little arm to her wrist, and led her to a chair, she being helpless against his giant strength.

"Nay," he said, "thou shan't tell him. It would half kill him first, and then he'd go and kill parson's boy."

"Yes, yes; he would, he would," sobbed Polly. "I dared not tell him, and it's been breaking my heart. But I won't bear it. Go away from here. How dare you say such things to me?"

"Howd thy tongue, lass," said Jock, in a deep growl, and his strong will mastered hers. "Hearken to me, Polly. I beg thy pardon, lass, and I can read it in thy pretty eyes that all I said was a lie. I beg thy pardon, lass."

"How could you—how dare you?" sobbed Polly. "Tom, Tom! come here—come here!"

"Hush! he can't hear thee, lass," growled Jock. "I've seen so much that I thought thou wast playing a bad game against Tom; but I was wrong, my little lass, and I say forgive me."

"Let me go and tell Tom all now," she sobbed. "I shan't be happy till I do."

"Dost want to mak' thyself happy," growled Jock, sinking into his old Lincolnshire brogue, after losing much by absence in other counties—"happy, half breaking Tom's heart, and getting murder done? If thou dost—go!"

Polly bounded to the door to seek her husband's help, and tell him all, Jock watching her the while; but as she reached the door her courage failed, and she turned away with a piteous wail.

"Oh, God help me!" she cried; "what shall I do?"

"Come and sit down, lass, and dry thy eyes," said Jock, kindly. "Say thou forgives me. I'm very sorry, lass. I'm a down bad un, but I like owd Tom. He's a good 'un, is Tom."

"The best, the truest of men."

"And I'm glad he's got a good little true wife," growled Jock. "There, it's all right, ain't it, Polly?" he said, taking her little hand in his and patting it. "Say thou forgives me."

"But—but you don't believe me," sobbed Polly.

"But I do," he said, kissing her little hand in a quiet, reverential way that ill accorded with his looks. "Say thou forgives me, lass."

"I do forgive you, Jock," she said, wiping her eyes. "Now let's call dear Tom in and tell him all."

"Nay," said Jock, "he mustn't be told. He's troubled enough as it is. I'll mak' it reight."

"No, no, Jock," cried Polly, with her cheeks turning like ashes.

"What, are you afraid I shall drownd him?" he said, sharply.

"Yes! Oh, it is so horrible!"

"Nay, I wean't drownd him if he'll keep away," said Jock, fiercely, "but I'll hev a word wi' him when he least expects it."

"I—I thought," faltered Polly, "that when he was married he would keep away."

"Nay, not he," growled Jock; "but I heven't done wi' him and his yet."

"But, Jock!"

"Get me some bread and cheese, lass," he growled, and she rose in a timid way, and gazing at him fearfully, spread a cloth, and placed the food before him.

"Now go and bathe thy pretty eyes," he said, as he sat down; "but stay a moment, lass."

He took both her hands in his, and drew her to him, and kissed her forehead.

"I beg thy pardon, Polly," he said once again; "and now go, and I promise that he shall never trouble thee again."

"But, Jock!"

"Howd thy tongue, lass. I wean't drown him, but if I don't scar him from this lane my name's not Jock."

Polly left the kitchen, and the great fellow sat there eating heartily for a time, and then Polly came back.

"Sometimes, lass," he said, "I think thou

ought to hev towd Tom all ; sometimes I don't. Wait a bit till that Serrol Mallow's gone again, and then tell him all. Hah! he's a nice 'un, and his brother too. They're gentlemen, they are. I'm on'y a rough shack. It mak's me laugh though, Polly. it do. I don't work, they say. Well, I don't see as they do, and as owd Bone used to mak' us read at school, nobody can't say as Jock Morrison, bad as he is, ever goes neighing after his neighbour's wife. Theer lass, theer lass, it's all put away, and I'm down glad as I was wrong."

" And you will frighten him away, Jock?" said Polly, who looked very bright and pretty now.

"That I will, Polly," said the great fellow, draining his mug; "and, my lass, I don't know but what Tom's reight to sattle down wi' such a pretty little lass as thou. Mebbe I shall be doing something of the sort myself. Good-bye, lass, good-bye."

"When when shall we see you again?" said Polly, in a timid way.

"Don't know, my lass, but I may be close at hand when no one sees me. I'm a curus, hiding sort of a fellow. Theer, good-bye."

He stooped and left the house, and Polly saw him go towards the workshop, stop talking for a few minutes, and then go slowly rolling along the lane.

"I'm afraid Jock's after no good, Polly, my little woman," said Tom quietly that night. "Ah, well, there's worse fellows than he."

"I like Jock better than ever I liked him before," cried Polly, with animation.

"I wish you could like him into a better life," said Tom, thoughtfully. "I wonder where the poor old chap has gone."

On a mission of his own. That very afternoon Cynthia had tempted her sister out of the solitude she so much affected now, by proposing a ride; for Lord Artingale had sent the horses over with a note saying that he had been called away to the county town, but would come over in the evening.

Julia took some pressing, but she agreed at last, the horses were brought round, and soon after the sisters mounted, and were cantering along the pleasant sandy lanes, followed some fifty yards or so behind by a well-mounted groom.

The sun shone brightly, and there was a deliciously fresh breeze, just sufficient to make the exercise enjoyable. The swift motion, with the breeze fanning her face, seemed to brighten Julia's eyes and send a flush into her cheeks, as they cantered on, Cynthia being full of merry remarks, and gladly noticing her sister's change.

"Oh, if she would only pluck up a little spirit," thought Cynthia; and then she began to wonder whether Artingale would bring over Magnus.

Then she began to make plans as to how she would bring them together, and leave them pretty often alone.

One way and another, as they rode on and on, Miss Cynthia mentally proved herself a very female Von Moltke in the art of warfare, and so wrapt was she in her thoughts, that she paid no heed to the fidgeting of the beautiful creature she was riding.

"Isn't your mare very tiresome, Cynthia?" said Julia.

"Only fresh, dear; I don't mind," was the reply. "I can manage her."

They were now in one of the winding, hilly lanes running through a series of the shaws or little woods common in that part of the country, and intersected by narrow rides for the convenience of the shooting parties and those who hunt. Everything looked very beautiful, and with her troubled breast feeling more at rest than it had for weeks, Julia was really enjoying her ride.

"Why, this is what we ought often to do," thought Cynthia. "Quiet, mare! Julia seems to feel safe from the ogre now she is well mounted. How pretty she looks!"

Julia certainly did look very beautiful just then, though she might have reciprocated the compliment. Her dark blue habit fitted her to perfection, her little glossy riding-hat was daintily poised upon her well-shaped head, and she rode her mare gracefully and well.

"Shall I take up a link or two of her curb, ma'am?" said the groom, cantering up, as Mad Sal seemed to be growing excited.

"Oh no, Thomas; she'll quiet down. It would only make her more fidgety. I'll give her a gallop."

If she had not decided to give it, Mad Sal would have taken it; for as she spoke and loosened her rein, the graceful creature sprang off at a gallop, and after a few strides began to go like the wind.

"Oh, Thomas, Thomas," cried Julia; "gallop!"

"Don't you be frightened, Miss," said the groom, smiling. "Miss Cynthia won't hurt. I never see a lady as could go like her. Shall I gallop after her, miss?"

"Yes, yes, quickly," cried Julia, excitedly: and, knowing the country, the groom turned his horse's head, put him at and leaped a low hedge into a field between two patches of coppice, and went off hunting fashion, to cut off a long corner round which he knew his young charge would go.

Julia hesitated about following, and then kept on at an easy canter along the road, following her sister's steps, till suddenly she turned ghastly pale, as, about fifty yards in front, she saw a man force his way through the low hedge, and then, evidently hot and panting with a long run, come towards her.

She had but to lash her mare and dash by him. She could have turned and cantered off with ease. But she did neither, merely sitting paralyzed, as it were, with her eyes fixed upon the great dark-bearded fellow, who came boldly up, laid his hand upon the rein, and the mare stopped short.

"Why, my beauty," he said, in a low deep voice, as he passed his arm through the rein, and placed his great hands upon the trembling girl's waist, "I thought I was never going to see you again."

Julia did not answer, though her lips parted as if to utter a cry.

"There," he said, "don't look frightened. I wouldn't hurt you for the world. I've got you safe, and the mare too. I don't know which is the prettiest. There, you're all right; they won't be back this half-hour. I've got you safe; jump!"

As he spoke he lifted her out of the saddle, and the next moment she was clasped tight in the fellow's arms—the dove quite at the mercy of the hawk.

CHAPTER X.

AT KILBY.

WINTER came in early that year, but none the less fiercely. Cyril and his young wife stayed on, Sage eagerly agreeing to her aunt's proposal that the visit should be prolonged, and consequently the rabbits on the farm had a very hard time, especially when the snow came, and their footprints could be tracked with ease.

John Berry brought his young wife and children, to the great delight of the Churchwarden, of whom they made a perfect slave, for he was never weary of petting them.

Lord Artingale came over once, and won golden opinions of Mrs. Portlock by what she called his condescension; and as to his nominee at the next election, the Churchwarden was ready to support him through thick and thin for the interest he took in Rue Berry's little children.

Harry Artingale was not the only gentleman visitor who found his way to the farm, for Frank Mallow came one evening soon after the Berrys had arrived, and that night, when Sage had gone up with her sister to her room, Rue suddenly burst into a hysterical fit of weeping.

"Why, Rue, darling," exclaimed her sister, "what is it?"

"Nothing, nothing at all," she cried hastily, wiping her eyes and cheering up. "Only one of my foolish fits, Sagey. There, there, good night."

"But you are ill," said Sage, anxiously.

"Ill, dear? No; it is only a little hysterical feeling that I have sometimes," and wishing her sister good night in the most affectionate manner, Sage left her bending over the little bedstead where her children slept, and as Sage closed the door she saw Rue sinking down upon her knees.

It was not a pleasant time, for Cyril had

grown short and sulky whenever Frank came, and seeing this, Frank laughed, and became unpleasantly attentive to his brother's young wife.

"If he won't be polite to you, Sage, I will," he cried. "I want you to have pleasant memories of me when I am gone."

"But are you going soon?" she asked.

"Oh, yes, I shall go soon," he replied; "I'm tired of this narrow country. Ah, Portlock, you should come with me."

"No, no," exclaimed Mrs. Portlock, excitedly. "My husband could not think of such a thing."

The Churchwarden, who was puffing away at his pipe when this was said, gave Frank Mallow a peculiar look, to which that gentleman nodded and stroked his dark beard.

"Well, I don't know, mother," he said; "farming's getting very bad here, and those who emigrate seem to do very well."

"Oh, no, Joseph; I don't believe they do," cried Mrs. Portlock, plaiting away at her apron, so as to produce the effect since become fashionable under the name of kilting.

"Why, look at young Luke Ross," said the Churchwarden; "he's emigrated to London, and they say getting on wonderful."

"Home's quite good enough for me, Joseph," said Mrs. Portlock, "and I wouldn't go on any consideration."

Frank Mallow took up the ball here, but the Churchwarden saw that Sage had turned pale and was bending over her work, so he stopped, and Frank went on painting the pictures of Australian life in the most highly-coloured style.

This visit became an extremely painful one to Sage, for, to Cyril's great annoyance, Frank came more and more, bantering his brother on his ill-humour, taking not the slightest notice of Mrs. Berry, who had turned very cold and reserved to him now, and evidently trying to pique her by his attentions to Sage.

The latter began to look upon him with horror, and dreaded Cyril's absences, which were very frequent, there always being something to shoot over at Gatley, or a trip to make somewhere; and at last it became almost a matter of course, as soon as Cyril had gone, for Frank to come sauntering in to have a chat with the Churchwarden upon sheep.

As a rule the Churchwarden would be absent, and Mrs. Portlock would begin to exert herself to make the visitor's stay comfortable, always contriving a little whispered conversation with him in the course of his visit, and begging him not to induce Portlock to emigrate. For it would be such a pity at his age, she whispered. And then, as soon as he got free, he would begin chatting to Sage, who sat there afraid to seem cold, but all the time being ill at ease, for a horrible suspicion had come over her, and fight against it how she would, she could not drive it away.

A great change had come over Rue, and it seemed to Sage so horrible, that she reproached herself for harbouring the idea that her sister's affection had come back for her old lover; that he was trying all he could to win her from her duty as a wife and mother; and that she, Sage, was being used as a blind to hide the real state of the case from her aunt and uncle. As for John Berry, there was no need to try and blind him, for in his simple, honest fashion he had the fondest trust in his wife; and if any one had hinted that she was falling away from him, if it had been a man, he would have struck him down.

A fortnight passed, and the frost still lasted. The Churchwarden, in his genial hospitality, said that it was a glorious time, but to Sage it was one of intense mental pain. Cyril had gone back to London, but was to come back and fetch her; but even if he had been there, Sage would have shrunk from speaking to him, seeing what a horrible accusation she would be making against her own sister and his brother; and she shrank from it the more from a dread of saying or doing anything to estrange Cyril, who had certainly been of late colder than his wont.

"Should she tell Julia?"

No, she seemed ill, and to avoid her now, and Sage was too proud to attempt to force herself upon her sister-in-law if she wished to keep away.

It was a terrible time for her, as she realized more and more, from various little things she saw, that Frank Mallow had, from old associations, regained his old power over Rue, and to her horror she felt certain that they had had stolen interviews.

"What should she do?" she asked herself; and now she wished that Cyril was back, for suddenly, just as Sage was praying that John Berry would make up his mind to go home, he announced his intention of going alone.

"It's bitter cold there after the place has been shut up, Churchwarden, and if thou does not mind I'll leave Rue and the little ones, and come over and fetch them in about a week's time."

Frank glanced at Sage, and their eyes met, sending a thrill of horror through the latter, as she felt more and more sure that her sister was growing weaker; and Sage closed her eyes, and bitterly reproached her husband for leaving her alone at such a time.

She formed a dozen plans, but rejected them all, and tried to invent others. She felt that she could not speak to her uncle and aunt; she dared not accuse her sister, for she was not sure, and hour after hour she was praying that she might have been deceived; but all the same she felt bound to act, and finally she determined that she would never leave Rue alone when Frank Mallow was in the house.

Sage's plan was good, but she could not keep to it; and one day, as she was about to enter the dining-room, where she had left her sister alone for a few moments, she heard her say, in a piteous voice—

"Oh, Frank, spare me! I cannot—I dare not!"

"It is too late now," he said. "All is arranged. You must!"

Sage did not enter the room, but stood there trembling as she heard her aunt go in by the farther door, and begin chattering to them both; but, with her blood seeming to run cold, she hurried up to her own room, and threw herself on her knees to pray for strength and wisdom at this crisis.

If she told her uncle or her aunt, the consequences seemed to be terrible. If she spoke to Rue, she foresaw that her sister would deny all.

She now determined what to do. She

would attack Frank himself, and insist upon his leaving the house at once, never to return; but on going down to put her plan into effect, she found that he was gone, and he did not return.

To her surprise, Rue seemed to have grown calmer now, and as the evening wore on she was almost cheerful, as if a load was off her mind.

Her equanimity almost disarmed Sage, and about eight o'clock, as they were sitting with their aunt and uncle, listening to the roaring of the wind, the precursor of a snow-storm, Sage sat quite still as her sister rose and said that she wanted to go up and see if the children were asleep.

Taking a candle, Rue lit it, and her face seemed very bright as she stood for a moment looking at the little party in the room.

"Let me see," said the Churchwarden; "I forgot to tell you, my dear. I saw the parson this afternoon. He had had a letter from Cyril."

"From Cyril?" cried Sage, eagerly.

"Yes, my dear; and he said it was just possible that he might be down to-night."

"And he did not write and tell me," thought Sage, as her sister left the room.

"It will be a roarer to-night," said the Churchwarden, as the wind howled in the broad chimney, and the soft dull patting noise of falling flakes could be heard upon the window-panes. "Shouldn't wonder if we had a power o' snow."

"And he did not write and say he was coming," thought Sage again, as a curious pang seemed to be followed by a dull aching in her breast.

"Ah!" continued the Churchwarden, tapping his pipe on the great dog-irons, and meditatively putting the burning wood together with his boot, "I thought it was coming, mother. We shall be snowed up safe. If Cyril Mallow is under a good roof anywhere, he'll stay there for the night, if he's got the brains I give him the credit for."

Just then a curious wailing noise made by the wind fell upon Sage's ear, and it seemed to her as if she had received a sudden shock, for from old associations with this her youthful home she knew what caused that sound—

the side door had been opened and softly closed.

Sage sat there for a few moments motionless, and felt as if turned to stone, for she knew, as surely as if she had seen it all, that her sister had opened that door and had gone to join Frank Mallow somewhere close at hand.

The terrible nightmare-like feeling passed off as quickly as it had come, and, how she hardly knew, Sage left the room, went straight to the side door, catching down her hat and cloak from the pegs, and passed out into the bitter night.

The wind nearly snatched the cloak from her as she flung it on, and then ran along the path towards the lane, for there were fresh footprints in the newly-fallen snow ; and so quickly did she run that at the end of ten minutes she was within sight of a dark figure hurrying on before her with bended head, and the driving snow rapidly making it invisible as it hurried on.

The storm was rapidly increasing, and the wind and drifting snow confused her ; but she ran on now, and with a despairing cry flung her arms round the figure, crying—

"Rue—sister! Where are you going? Oh, for heaven's sake, stop!"

"Sage!" she cried, hoarsely, and she struggled to free herself; but Sage clung to her tightly, and she stumbled, slipping on the hard ground beneath the snow, and sinking to her knees.

Sage knelt beside her upon the snow, and, clasping her waist, she sobbed—

"Yes, yes, upon your knees, Rue—sister, pray, pray with me—for strength. God hear our cry, and save my sister from this sin!"

For a few moments, as she heard the passionate cry, Rue knelt there trembling, but she began to struggle again.

"Don't stop me. It is too late now. I cannot help it, Sage; I must go."

"You shall not go. I know all. He has tempted you to do this wrong, and you are mad; but think—for God's sake, think. It will break John's heart."

"Oh, hush, hush!" Rue cried, with a shiver. "Hush, hush! I must go now!"

"You shall not; I will never leave you. Rue, dear, there are two little children lying there in their bed, silently calling you to come to them and avoid this sin. Sister—mother—wife, will you leave them for that cruel, reckless man?"

"Oh, hush!" cried Rue, struggling with her fiercely. "You do not know. You cannot tell. He's waiting for me, and I must—I will go."

"Never while I have breath," Sage panted, and then she uttered a shriek of affright, for Rue made an effort to escape her, running for some distance, and then falling heavily in the snow.

This was her last struggle, for as Sage overtook her, the weak woman rose, and, trembling and moaning to herself, she allowed her sister to lead her back towards the farm.

How Sage managed to get her sister along she never afterwards knew, but by degrees she did, and up to her room unheard, hiding away all traces of the snowy cloaks and boots before summoning Mrs. Portlock to her help, for as soon as Rue reached the bedroom she threw herself upon her knees by her sleeping children, moaning, sobbing, speaking incoherently, and passing from one terrible hysterical fit into another that seemed worse.

"Go and tell uncle she's better now," said Mrs. Portlock, at last; "I can hear him walking up and down like a wild beast. There, there, now, my child," she said soothingly to Rue, "try and be calm."

Sage went down to find the Churchwarden buttoned up and with the old horn lanthorn lit, ready to walk over to the town and fetch Doctor Vinnicombe.

"I'm afraid it's no use to put a horse to, my dear," he said; "the snow's drifting tremendously."

"I don't think you need go, uncle," said Sage, and here she stopped short and clung to him, for there was a sharp knocking at the front door, and in her confused, excited state Sage's heart sank, for she felt that it was Frank Mallow grown impatient, and come to insist upon Rue keeping her word.

"There, there, my pretty, don't you turn silly too," said the Churchwarden. "By jingo, what a night!" he cried, as the outer door was opened, and a rush of snow-laden wind swept into the hall and dashed open the big parlour door.

The sound of a rough voice gave Sage relief, for it was John Berry who had arrived.

The relief was but momentary, for Sage's conscience said that the husband had gained some inkling of the intended flight, and had come to stop it.

Just then the broad-shouldered, red-faced farmer entered the room.

"How are ye?" he cried in a bluff tone that set Sage's heart at rest for the moment. "I scarcely thought the mare would have got me through it," he continued. "It's a strange rough night, master, and if you've any sheep out, I'd have 'em seen to. Eh? what? My darling ill?" he cried, as he heard the Churchwarden's announcement. "Then thank the Lord I did come."

"No, no; don't go to her now," panted Sage, as John Berry took off his coat and threw it out into the hall.

"Not go up to her? Nay, lass, that I

will," he cried, and Sage followed him up-stairs.

" Why, Rue, my lass," he cried, tenderly. " what's wrong wi' you ? "

At the sound of his voice Rue started from the bed and flung herself into his arms.

" Jack, Jack ! " she cried, " take me—hold me—husband, dear.   God have mercy on me ! I must be mad."

Sage stayed with them in obedience to a sign from John Berry, and stood there trembling as she saw her sister's fair brown hair tumbled upon her husband's breast, to which she clung in an agony of remorse.

Over and over again Rue kept raising her head, though to gaze piteously at her sister, and then hide her face again.

A couple of hours went on like this, but when at last Sage found her opportunity, and clasping her sister to her breast, whispered—

" Rue, may I trust you now ? "

" Yes, oh, yes," she sobbed. " I pray God I may never see his face again."

" Then that is our secret, Rue," Sage whispered. " It is for ever buried in our breasts."

She left them after some hours, Rue lying upon the bed, sobbing at times, and seemingly asleep, while John Berry sat beside her, holding her little white hands.

Sage went down softly, but began to tremble as she heard voices in the room; but summoning up her courage, she entered, to find Morrison, the wheelwright, standing there, with the Churchwarden placing a glass of hot spirits and water in his hand.

"Go back, go back, my darling," cried Mrs. Portlock, excitedly.

"No, no, my dear," said the Churchwarden, firmly; "Sage is no coward, and she must know. My darling, try and be firm, and hope for the best. The cart will be here directly, and we're going to force our way through and bring him in. Yes, there it comes."

"What—what is it?" panted Sage. "Is—is Frank——"

"Oh, pray be silent, Joseph," sobbed Mrs. Portlock.

"Why?" said the Churchwarden, firmly. "She must know the worst. Get hot water and blankets ready, my dear, and we'll soon bring him round. Come, Morrison," and hurrying out, the door was pushed to, forcing back with it a quantity of the soft white snow.

"For heaven's sake tell me, aunt!" sobbed Sage.

"But am I to?" said the old lady, trembling before her niece.

"Yes, yes," cried Sage. "I must know. Is he dead?"

"No, no, my darling," said Mrs. Portlock, piteously. "Tom Morrison was going home, but he could not get round by the ford. The cutting in Low Lane was full, so he came round our way; and—oh, dear me! oh, dear me!"

"For heaven's sake, aunt, go on," cried Sage, half fiercely now.

"Yes, my darling," sobbed Mrs. Portlock; "and they'll be here directly, I hope and pray. And he came upon Cyril."

"Cyril!" shrieked Sage.

"Lying buried in the snow, just at the corner where he fought Luke Ross."

Sage stood gazing at her with a blank white face, shivering violently as her aunt went on in a voice choked with tears.

"Tom Morrison tried to carry him on here, but he could not get him through the snow, so he came for help, and—heaven be thanked, here they are!"

The room seemed to swim round Sage as she heard the sound of voices above the roaring of the wind, and going with her aunt and the two affrighted servants to the door, they stood their ground in spite of the beating and driving snow, till a stiffened white figure was borne into the great parlour and laid before the fire, the Churchwarden giving orders in all directions.

"We could never get Vinnicombe across to-night, so we must bring him round ourselves. Quick, every one. Hot blankets, and let's get these snowy things away. Why in God's name don't some one shut that door?' he roared, as the wind and snow followed them into the room, making the fire roar furiously and the sparks stream up.

"Don't be downhearted," cried the Churchwarden, setting the example, as John Berry came in to see what was the matter.

"Hey, and what is it?" he said, laying his hand upon the wheelwright's arm.

"Mr. Cyril Mallow, Master Berry; we found him in the snow."

It was just as Sage's heart gave a great bound of relief, for as the mist cleared from her eyes and the giddiness passed away, she found herself kneeling beside her husband's brother, frozen stiff where he had been waiting for hours at the trysting-place. And as Sage gazed with a strange feeling of awe at the stern white features set in death, the Church-warden said softly, "Nay, Morrison, thou'rt wrong, my lad; it is Mr. Frank. He must have been coming here."

CHAPTER XI.

LOVERS' WORDS.

TIME flies.

Not an original remark this, but perfectly true.

Decorous mourning had been worn for Frank Mallow, the invalid mother had grown more grey, and the lines in her forehead deeper, while as the Rector thought of the fate of his firstborn, and shut his ears to little bits of scandal that floated about, he sighed, and turned more and more to his daughters, for Cyril, fortunately for himself, had quite forsaken Lawford since his brother's death, having troubles of his own to contend with, while his wife had hers.

Rue Berry's adventure remained a secret

between the sisters, and though at the weekly meetings at the King's Head there were a good many nods and shakes of the head as to the reason why, on the night of his death, Frank Mallow had engaged a fly and pair of horses, such matter was never openly discussed, Tomlinson sagely remarking that when a man died there was a thick black mark ruled across the page of his ledger, and it was not worth while to tot up an account that there was no one to pay.

Then, as time went on, the inquest was forgotten, and the tablet placed in the church by the Rector, sacred to the memory of Frank, the beloved son, etcetera, etcetera, only excited notice during one weekly meeting, when Fullerton wondered what had become of the fortune Frank Mallow had made in Australia.

His fellow-tradesmen wondered, and so did Cyril Mallow to such an extent that he borrowed a hundred pounds from Portlock the churchwarden to pay for investigations and obtain the money.

" Seed corn, mother," said Portlock, grimly ; " seed corn for Cyril Mallow to sow ; but hang me, old lady, if I believe it will ever come to a crop."

As soon as possible after the terrible shock Mrs. Mallow had received, the Rector took her abroad, and for eight months they were staying at various German baths, changing from place to place, the Rector now and then—handsome, grey-bearded, and the very beau ideal of an English clergyman—drawing large congregations when he occupied the pulpit of the chaplain at some foreign watering-place.

It was a pleasant time of calm for him, and he sighed as he thought of returning to England; but this return was fast approaching for many reasons. One reason was the Bishop. Certainly the Rev. Lawrence Paulby was indefatigable with the business of the church. but the Bishop seemed to agree in spirit with the meeting at the King's Head, that it was not quite right for one clergyman to draw fifteen hundred a year from a parish and not do the duty, while another clergyman only drew ninety pounds a year and did do the duty, and did it well.

Another reason was, both Lord Artingale

and Perry-Morton had been over again and again, and after a decent interval had pressed hard for their marriages to take place.

The last visit had been to a popular place of resort, where poor Mrs. Mallow was, by the advice of the German physician, undergoing a process of being turned into an aqueous solution; at least she was saturated daily with an exceedingly nauseous water, and soaked in it hot for so many hours per week as well. The same great authority recommended it strongly for Julia, who drank the waters daily to the sound of a band. He also advised that the Fraulein Cynthia should take a lesser quantity daily also, to the strains of the German band, at intervals of promenading; but Cynthia merely took one sip and made a pretty grimace, writing word afterwards that the "stuff" was so bad that if the servants at home had been asked to use it to wash their hands there would have been a revolt.

There were other reasons too for calling back the Rev. Eli Mallow, and he sighed, for it was very pleasant abroad, and he foresaw trouble upon his return—parish trouble, the worry of the weddings. contact with Cyril. with whom he had quarrelled bitterly by letter, refusing to furnish him with money, a fact which came hard upon Churchwarden Portlock, who bore it like a martyr, and smoked more pipes as, for some strange reason, he raked up and dwelt strongly upon every scrap of information he could obtain about the progress of Luke Ross in London, even going over to the market-place occasionally to have a pipe and a chat with old Michael his father.

There was no help for it, and at last the luggage was duly packed, and after poor Mrs Mallow had been carefully carried down, the family started for home, and settled for the time being in one of a handsome row of houses north of the park.

"Yes, my dear, it is—very expensive," said the Rector, in answer to a remark, almost a remonstrance, from the invalid; "but we must keep up appearances till the girls are married. Then, my dear. we shall be alone, and we will go down to the old home, and there will be nothing to interfere with our quiet, peaceful journey to the end."

Mrs. Mallow turned her soft pensive eyes up to him as he leaned over the couch, and he bent down and kissed her tenderly.

"Well, my darling, who can say?" he whispered. "If more trouble comes, it is our fate, and we will try and bear the burden as best we can."

"But you will go down now and then to Lawford, Eli?" she said, and the Rector sighed.

"Yes, my dear, I will," he said; "but at present we must stay in town." And he placed his hands behind him and walked up and down the room, wishing that he could understand the Lawford people, or that they could understand him, and looking forward with anything but pleasurable anticipations to his next visit.

Just then Julia, looking very pale and dreamy in her half-mourning, entered the room, to come and sit with and read to the invalid, a visitor being below, and her presence not being in any way missed.

Henry, Lord Artingale was the visitor, and as soon as she had left the room Julia became one of the principal topics, for she had seemed of late to have fallen into a dreamy state, now indifferent, now reckless, and Cynthia declared pettishly that she gave her sister up in despair.

"I don't know what to make of her, Harry," said Cynthia one morning after they had been back in town some time; "one day she will be bright and cheerful, another she seems as if she were going melancholy mad."

"Oh, no; come, that's exaggeration, little one."

"It is not," cried Cynthia, "for she is wonderfully changed when we are together."

"How changed? Why, she looks prettier than ever."

"I mean in her ways," continued Cynthia. "We used to be sisters indeed, and never kept anything from one another. Why, Harry, I don't believe either of us had a thought that the other did not share, and now I seem to be completely shut out from her confidence; and if it were not for you, I believe I should break my heart."

Of course Harry Artingale behaved as a manly handsome young fellow should behave under such circumstances. He comforted and condoled with the afflicted girl, who certainly did not look in the slightest degree likely to break her heart. He offered his manly bosom for her to rest her weary head, and he removed the little pearly tears from under the pretty fringed lids of her large bright eyes. There were four of them—tears, not eyes—and Harry wiped them away without a pocket-handkerchief, the remains of one damaged tear remaining on his moustache when the process was over, and poor little Cynthia seemed much better.

"Well," said Artingale, "there is one comfort, Cynthy: we did scare away the big bogey. She has not seen him any more?"

"No—no!" said Cynthia softly, "I suppose not. She has never said anything about him since we were at Hastings. I have fancied sometimes that she has seen him and been frightened; but she never mentions it, and I have always thought it best never to say a word."

"Oh, yes, far the best," said Artingale, who was examining Cynthia's curly hair with as much interest as if it was something he saw now for the first time. "Didn't you say, though, that you thought she saw him that day the mare bolted with you?"

"Nonsense! she did not bolt with me, Harry. Just as if I should let a mare bolt with me. Something startled her, and she leaped the hedge, and as we were off the road. and it was a chance for a gallop, I let her go across country. But you know; I told you."

"Yes, dear," said Artingale, one of whose fingers was caught in a sunny maze. "But now, Cynthy, my pet, *revenons à nos moutons.*"

"Very well, sir," she said shyly, "*revenons à nos moutons.*"

"So the wedding is to be on the fourth?"

"Yes," said Cynthia, with a sigh, "on the fourth—not quite a month, Harry. Where's James Magnus?"

"Shut up in his studio, splashing the paint about like a madman. He never comes out hardly He has cut me, and spends most of his time with that barrister fellow who was to have married Sage Portlock."

Luke Ross! Oh! Are they friends?"

"Thick as thieves," said Artingale. "I

suppose they sit and talk about disappointed love, and that sort of thing."

"Do they?" cried Cynthia.

"Oh, I don't know, of course. By Jove, though, Cynthy, that Ross is a splendid fellow; no one would ever have thought he was only a tanner's son."

"I don't see what difference it makes whose son a man is," said Cynthia, demurely. "I've always noticed though that poor people's sons are very clever, and noblemen's sons very stupid."

"Horribly," said Artingale, laughing. "Why, you saucy little puss!"

Matters here not necessary for publication.

"I don't want to say unkind things," said Cynthia, pouting now, "but I'm sure poor Sage Portlock would have been a great deal wiser if she had married Luke Ross; and if you were in your right senses, Harry, you would never think of marrying into such an unhappy family as ours."

"Oh, but then I've been out of my mind for long enough, Cynthy. The wise ones said I ran mad after the Rector's little daughter."

"When you might have made a most brilliant match or two, I heard," cried Cynthia.

"Yes, pet, all right," he said, laughing; "but you're in for it. I won't be pitched over."

"I'm sure the state of Cyril's home is disgraceful."

"I dare say, my darling; but we are not going to live there."

"Don't be so stupid," cried Cynthia. "But tell me, Harry, has James Magnus cut you?"

"No. Oh, no; only I am so much away now that instead of being regular chums we don't often meet. Hah! what jolly times I used to have with him, to be sure!"

"I hate him," cried Cynthia, angrily. "He's a great stupid coward."

"No, you don't, Cynthy; and you don't think he is a coward."

"Well, perhaps I don't hate him very much, and perhaps I don't think him a very great coward; but, oh! Harry, if I had been a man, do you think I would have allowed that miserable—miserable——"

"Design for a wall-paper or fresco?" suggested Artingale.

"Yes, yes, yes," cried Cynthia, laughing and clapping her hands with childlike delight. "That's it: what a grand idea! Oh, Harry, how clever you are!"

She looked up at him admiringly, and he smiled, and—— Well, of course, that was sure to follow. Young lovers are so very foolish, and it came natural to them to tangle one another up in their arms, and for Cynthia's nose to be hidden by Artingale's moustache.

Then they grew *sage*, as the French call it, once more, and Artingale spoke—

"That's right, little pet, think so if you can; but I wish, for your sake, I were——"

"Were what, sir?"

"Clever. Do you know, Cynthy, I often think what a good job it was that nature had the property valued before I was launched."

"Why, you dear stupid old boy, what do you mean?"

"What I say, pet: had me valued. Then he said, 'Well, he's got no brains, and he'll never do any good for himself if he is left alone ; so I'll make him a lord and give him an income.' "

" Oh, Harry, what nonsense ! "

" And then, to help me on a bit farther when I had grown to years of indiscretion, she gave me, or is about to give me, the dearest and best and sweetest and most beautiful of little women to be my wife."

Which was, of course, very stupid again ; and more resulted, after which Artingale said quietly—

" Cynthy, dear, you believe in me thoroughly ? "

" Thoroughly, Harry."

" You know I love you with all my heart ? "

" Yes, Harry," she replied, with her hands in his.

" Then you will not think me strange if I say to you I don't want to be married yet ? "

" N—no," said Cynthia, with just a suspicion of hesitation.

" Then I'm going to speak out plainly, darling. I'm stupid in some things, but I'm as sharp as a needle concerning anything

about you, and I couldn't help seeing that the
Rector and mamma thought that our wed-
ding might take place at the same time as
Julia's."

"Ye—es," faltered Cynthia.

"Well, then," said Artingale, "I would
rather for several reasons it did not."

He waited for a few moments, but Cynthia
did not speak.

"I'm not going to talk nonsense about
being like brothers," he continued, "and
loving James Magnus; but, Cynthy, dear, I
never yet met a man whom I liked half so
well, and—and I'd do anything for poor old
Jemmy. Well," he continued, "for one thing,
it seems horrible to me to make that the hap-
piest day of my life which will be like that
which kills his last hope."

Cynthia did not speak, but nestled closely
to him.

"Then it gives me a sensation like having a
cold douche to think of going up the church
with that fellow, for I know he'll be dressed
up like a figure in an old picture, with his
sisters and friends like so many animated pre-

Raphaelites in an idyllic procession attending the funeral of a fay."

"I say, Harry," cried Cynthia, "that's not your language, sir. Where did you pick it up?"

"Oh, out of Perry-Morton's new poems, as he called them. 'Pon my word, you know, I should feel as if it was a sort of theatrical performance. Oh, Cynthy, I should like to have you in white, and take you by the hand, and walk into some out-of-the-way little church in the country, where there was a nice, pleasant old parson, who'd read the service and say God bless us both ; and then for us to go away—right away, where all was green fields and flowers, and birds singing, and all the confounded nonsense and fuss and foolery of a fashionable wedding was out of my sight ; and——Cynthy, darling, let's make a runaway match of it, and go and be married to-morrow—to-day—now ; or let's wait till poor Julia has been sold. There, pet, hang it all ! it makes me wild."

He jumped up and began to pace the room, and Cynthia went up to him and put her arm through his.

"Harry, dear," she said softly, "you've made me very happy by what you have told me. Let's wait, dear. I should not like to be married then. I should like—should like—" she faltered, with her pretty little face burning—" our wedding to be all happiness and joy; and on the day when Julia is married to Perry-Morton, I shall cry ready to break my heart."

CHAPTER XII.

LAMBENT LOVE.

A CERTAIN small world, of which Mr. Perry-Morton was one of the shining lights, was deeply agitated, moved to its very volcanic centre, and gave vent to spasmodic utterances respecting the approaching marriage of their apostle to Julia, eldest daughter of the Rev. Eli Mallow, Rector of Lawford. There were no less than four paragraphs in as many papers concerning the bride's *parure* and *trousseau*, and the presents she was receiving.

"But I thought it would have excited more notice," said the Rev. Eli, mildly, after a discussion with the invalid, wherein he had firmly maintained his intention not to invite Cyril and his wife to the wedding.

The papers devoted to art gave a description of the interior of Mr. Perry-Morton's new mansion in Westminster, and dwelt at great length upon the artistic furnishing, and the additions being made of art tapestry, carpets, and curtains manufactured by the well-known firm of Gimpsley and Stough, from the designs of Smiless, A.R.A., and the wealthy bridegroom himself. The golden beetle conventionally treated was the leading *motif* in all the designs, and a yellow silk of a special orange-golden hue had been prepared for the purpose, the aniline dye being furnished by Judd, Son and Company. The carpets were so designed that on at-home nights the guests would be standing in the midst of gorgeous bugs, as an American friend termed them —beetles whose wings seemed to be moving beneath the feet of those who trod thereon. But the great feature of the salon was the central ottoman, which was a conventional rendering of a bank of flowers supporting golden beetles, amidst which were a few places upon which the so-inclined might rest and fancy the insects were alive.

Columns of chat were written in praise of Perry-Morton and his place, and copies of the papers in which they were, somehow found their way into a great many houses through the length and breadth of the land.

There was only one drawback to the joys of the stained-glass sisters, as they showed their friends through the house, and posed in graceful attitudes all over the carpets and against the hangings, in whose folds they almost wrapped themselves in their sweetly innocent delight—there was only one drawback, and that was, that another season was gliding by, and they were still on the matrimonial house-agents' books—these two eligible artistic *cottages ornées* to let.

Stay: there was another drawback. When dear Perry was married they would have to go, for unless dearest Julia pressed them very, very much indeed to continue their residence there, of course they could not stay.

These were busy times for Perry-Morton, who, in addition to the almost herculean labours which he went through in planning and designing, so as to make his home worthy of his goddess, had to beam every evening in Parkleigh Gardens.

This beaming was a very beautiful performance. Some men love with their eyes and look languishing, dart passionate glances, or seem to ask questions or sympathy from the fair one of their worship. Others, more manly and matter-of-fact, love with their tongues, and if clever in the use of this speaking organ, these generally woo and win, for most women love to be conquered by one who is their master in argument and pleading. There are others, again, who do not woo at all, but allow themselves to be fished for, hooked, and—and—what shall we say? There —cooked, for there is no more expressive way of describing their fate.

But Perry-Morton was none of those. He was like the Archduke in the French comic opera, nothing unless he was original; and it was only reasonable to suppose that he would bring his great artistic mind to bear upon so important a part of his life as the choice of an Eve for his modern-antique paradise. He did his wooing, then, in a way of his own, and came nightly to beam upon the object of his worship.

This he did in attitudes of his own designing, while Cynthia felt as if, to use her own words, she should like to stick pins in the man's back.

For Perry-Morton's love seemed to emanate from him in a phosphorescent fashion. He became lambent with softly luminous smiles. His plump face shone with a calm ethereal satisfaction, and of all men in the world he seemed most happy.

He did not trouble Julia much, only with his presence. He would lay a finger on the back of her chair, and pose himself like a sculptor's idea of one of the fat gods in the Greek Pantheon — say Bacchus, before too much grape-juice had begun to interfere with the proper working of his digestive organs. Or before the first wanderings of his very severe attacks of D. T., which must have caused so much consternation and dismay in Olympus' pleasant groves, and bothered Æsculapius, who applied leeches, because he would not own to his ignorance of the new disease.

He never kissed Julia once, so Cynthia declared. It is open to doubt whether he ever pressed her hand. His was the kiss-the-hem-of-the-lady's-garment style of love, and he once terribly alarmed Julia by gracefully reclining at her feet, with one arm resting upon a footstool, and gazing blandly in her face.

At other times he seemed to love her from a distance—getting into far-off corners of the room, and gazing from different points of view, standing, sitting, lying on sofas—always gracefully and in the most sculpturesque fashion. In fact, Artingale in great disgust wondered why he did not try standing on his head : but that was absurd.

As the day fixed for the wedding drew near, Perry-Morton was most regular in his visits—most devoted, and his lambent softness seemed to pervade the parental drawing-rooms.

Meanwhile Julia went about like one in a dream. She was less hysterical and timid than she had been for many weeks past, and finding that her lover troubled her so little, she bore his presence patiently, delighting him, as he confided to Cynthia, by her "heavenly calm."

"I don't think she's well," said Cynthia, shortly.

"Not well?" he said, with a pitying smile. "My sweet Cynthia, you cannot read her character as I read it. Do you not see how, for months past, our love has grown, rising like some lotus out from the cool depths of an Eastern lake till it has reached the surface, where it is about to unfold its petals to the glowing sun. Ah, my sweet child, you do not see how I have been forming her character, day by day, hour by hour, till she has reached to this sweet state of blissful repose. Look at her now."

This conversation was going on in the back drawing-room, on the evening preceding the wedding-day, every one being very tired of the visitors and congratulations, and present-giving, the Rector especially, and he confided to Mrs. Mallow the fact that after all he would be very glad to get away back to Lawford and be at peace.

"Yes," said Cynthia, rather ill-humouredly, for Harry had not been there that evening, "I see her, and she looks very poorly."

"Poorly? Unwell? Nay," said Perry-Morton serenely, "merely in a beatific state of repose. Ah, Cynthia, my child, when she is my very own, and Claudine has imparted to her some of the riches of her own wisdom on the question of dress, I shall be a happy man."

Cynthia seemed to give every nerve in her little body a kind of snatch, but the lover did not perceive it; he only closed his eyes, walked to the half-pillar that supported the arch between the two rooms, leaned his shoulder against it, crossed his legs, gazed at poor listless Julia for a few moments from this point of view, and then turning his half-closed eyes upon Cynthia, beckoned to her softly to come.

"Oh," whispered the latter to herself, as she drew a long breath between her teeth. "I wish I were going to be married to him to-morrow instead of Julia. How I would bring him to his senses, or knock something into his dreadful head, or—there, I suppose I must go. Julia must be mad."

"Yes," she said, as she crossed to where her brother in prospective stood.

"There," he said; "look now. Could there be a sweeter ideal of perfect repose? Good—good night, dear Cynthia. I am going to steal away without a word to a soul. I would not break in upon her rapturous calm; and the memory of her sweet face, as I see it now, will soothe me during the long watches of the peaceful night. Good night, Cynthia. Ah, you should have changed names. Yonder is Cynthia in all her calm silvery beauty. Good night, sweet sister—good night—good night."

There was something very moonlike in his looks and ways as he softly stole from the room and out of the house, leaving Cynthia motionless with astonishment.

"I want to know," she said to herself at last, "whether those two are really going to be married to-morrow, or whether it is only a dream. But there, I wash my hands of it all; I feel to-night as if I hate everybody—papa, mamma, Harry for not killing that horrible jelly-fish of a creature. Oh, he's dreadful! And Julia, for letting herself be led as she is, when she might have married dear James Magnus, and been happy. No! poor girl, I must not blame her. She felt that she could not love him, and perhaps she is right."

"Good night, Julia darling; I'm going to bed," she whispered, and, seating herself by her sister, she clasped her waist, and placed her lips against her cheek.

"To bed? so soon?" said Julia, dreamily.

"Soon! It is past eleven. Will you come and sit with me in my room, or shall I come to you?"

Julia shook her head.

"Not to-night—not to-night," she said softly; and she clasped her sister in her arms. "Good night, Cynthia dear. Think lovingly of me always when I am gone."

"Lovingly, Julie, always," whispered Cynthia; "always, dear sister."

"Always — whatever comes?" whispered Julia.

"Always, whatever comes. Shall I come and sit with you, Julie; only for an hour?"

"No," said Julia, firmly, "not to-night. Let us go to our rooms."

They went out of the drawing-room with their arms round each other's waists, till they were about to part at Julia's door, when the final words and appeals that Cynthia was about to speak died away upon her lips, and she ran to her own chamber, sobbing bitterly, while, white as ashes, and trembling in every limb, Julia entered hers.

"Poor, poor Julie!" sobbed Cynthia; and for a good ten minutes she wept, her maid snifling softly in sympathy till she was dismissed.

"Go away, Minson," cried Cynthia; "I don't want you any more."

"But won't you try on your dress again, miss?" said the maid in expostulation.

"No, Minson, I only wish it was fresh mourning, I do," cried the girl, passionately; and the maid withdrew, to meet Julia's maid on the stairs, and learn that she never knew such a thing before in her life—a young bride, and wouldn't try on her things.

Cynthia sat thinking for a few minutes, and then a bright look came into her eyes.

"He didn't come to-night," she said. "He was cross about Julie. I wonder whether I could see the bright end of a cigar if I looked out over the gardens. Oh, the cunning of some people, to give policemen half-sovereigns not to take them for burglars, and lock them up."

As she spoke, Cynthia drew up her blind softly, and holding back the curtain, ensconced herself in the corner, so that she could look down into the gardens, her window being towards the park.

It was a soft, dark night, but the light of a lamp made the objects below dimly distinct, and she rubbed the window-pane to gaze out more clearly, saying laughingly to herself—

"I wonder whether Romeo will come!"

Directly after she pressed her face closer to the glass.

"There he is," she said, with a gleeful little laugh. "No it isn't, I'm sure. What does it mean? What is he doing there?"

CHAPTER XIII.

AN EVENTFUL NIGHT.

"I can't go, and I won't go," said Artingale.
"It's bad enough to have to be at the church
to-morrow and see that poor little lass sacri-
ficed, with everybody looking on smiling and
simpering except the bridesmaids, who are all
expected to shed six tears.

"Six tears each, and six bridesmaids; that's
thirty-six tears. I'd almost bet a fiver that
those two pre-Raphaelite angels will each be
provided with an antique lachrymatory designed by their dear brother, and they'll drop
their tears therein and stopper them up.

"Oh, dear! This is a funny world, and I'm
very fond of my pretty Cynthy, who's a regular
little trump; but I'm getting deuced hungry.

I'll go and hunt up old Mag, and we'll have a bit of dinner together, and then go to the play. Liven him up a bit, poor old man. Hansom!"

A two-wheeled hawk swooped down, and carried him off to the studio of James Magnus, where that gentleman was busy with a piece of crayon making a design for a large cartoon-like picture, and after a good deal of pressing he consented to go to the club and dine with his friend.

"I'm afraid you'll find me very dull company," said Magnus, sadly.

"Then I'll make you lively, my boy. I'm off duty to-night, and I feel like a jolly bachelor. Champagne; coffee afterwards, and unlimited cigars."

"What a boy you are, Harry!" said the artist, quietly. "How you do seem to enjoy life!"

"Well, why shouldn't I? Plenty of troubles come that one must face; why make others?"

"Is — is she to be married to-morrow, Harry?" said Magnus, quietly.

"I say, hadn't we better taboo that subject, old fellow?" said Artingale, quickly.

"No. Why should we? Do you think I am not man enough to hear it calmly?"

Artingale looked at him searchingly.

"Well, yes, I hope so; and since you have routed out the subject, I suppose I must answer your question. Yes, she is, and more blame to you."

"We will not discuss that, Harry," said the other, sadly. "I know well enough that it was not in me to stir a single pulse in Julia Mallow's veins, and I have accepted my fate. Are you going to the wedding?"

"Yes: I feel that I must. But I hate the whole affair. I wish the brute would break his neck. Ready?"

"Yes," was the reply; and going out to the waiting hansom, they were soon run down to the club, where the choicest little dinner Artingale could select was duly placed before them.

But somehow, nothing was nice. Artingale's hunger seemed to have departed, and he followed his friend's example, and ate mechanically. The dry sherry was declared to be watery, and the promised champagne, though a choice brand and from a selected *cuvée*, was not able to transmit its sparkle to the brains of those who partook.

Artingale talked hard and talked his best. He introduced every subject he could, but in vain, and at last, when the time had come for the claret, he altered his mind.

"No, Mag," he exclaimed, "no claret to-night. We want nothing calm and cool, old fellow. I feel as if I had not tasted a single glass of wine, but as if you, you miserable old wet blanket, had been squeezing out your drops into a tumbler and I had been drinking them. What do you say to a foaming beaker of the best black draught?"

"My dear Harry, I'm very sorry," said Magnus, laughing. "There, I'll try and be a little more lively."

"We will," exclaimed Artingale, "and another bottle of champagne will do it."

Magnus smiled.

"Ah, smile away, my boy, but I'm going to give you a new sensation. I've made a discovery of a new wine. No well-known, highly-praised brand made famous by advertisements, but a rich, pungent, powerful. sparkling champagne, from a vineyard hardly known. Here, waiter, bring me a bottle of number fifty-three."

The wine was brought, and whether its virtues were exaggerated or no, its effects were that for the next two hours life seemed far more bearable to James Magnus, who afterwards enjoyed his coffee and cigar.

Then another cigar was partaken of, and another, after which it was found to be too late for the projected visit to one of the theatres, and Magnus proposed an adjournment to his own room.

To this, however, Artingale would not consent, and in consequence they sat till long after ten, and then parted, each to his own chambers.

Artingale's way of going to his own chambers was to take a hansom, and tell the man to drive him to the Marble Arch, and then along the Bayswater-road until told to stop.

This last order came before Kensington Gardens were reached, when the man was dismissed, and the fare wandered down the nearest turning, and along slowly by the backs of the Parkleigh Gardens houses—or their fronts, whichever the part was termed that faced north.

Up and down here he paraded several times—not a very wise proceeding, seeing that he might have come sooner in the evening, and the doors would have flown open at his summons. But it has always been so from the beginning. A gentleman gets into a certain state, and then thinks that he derives a great deal of satisfaction in gazing at the casket which holds the jewel of his love. When the custom first came in it is of course impossible to say, but it is extremely probable that Jacob used to parade about in the sand on moonlight nights, and watch the tent that contained his Rachel, and no doubt the custom has followed right away down the corridors of time.

When Artingale had finished the front of the house he went round to the back, made his way by some mysterious means into the garden, where he fancied he saw some one watching; and concluding that it would not be pleasant to be seen, he beat a retreat, and after a glance up at Cynthia's window, where he could see a light, he contented himself by walking slowly back, so as to get to the other side of the lofty row of houses.

"Just one walk up and down," he said to himself, "and then home to bed."

It was some distance round, and as he went along he made the following original observation :—

"This is precious stupid!"

And at the end of another fifty yards—

"But somehow I seem to like it. Does one good. 'Pon my soul, I think the best thing a fellow can do is to fall in love."

He sauntered on from gas-lamp to gas-lamp, till he was once more at the front, or back, of the great houses, with their entrance-doors on his right, and a great blank-looking wall on his left.

He went dreamily on along the pavement, past the furnished house that the agent assured the Rector he had obtained dirt cheap, which no doubt it was, but it was what a gold-miner would call wash dirt.

When about midway, Artingale passed

some one on the other side, close to the wall, and walking in the opposite direction.

But the presence of some one else in the street did not attract Artingale's attention, and he sauntered along until he reached the end, and stopped.

" Now, then," he said, " home ? or one more walk to the end and back ?"

He hesitated for a moment, and then turned beneath the lamp-post, with a smile at his own weakness, and walked slowly back.

" I should have made a splendid *Romeo*," he said. " What a pity it is that the course of my true love should run so jolly smooth. Everything goes as easy as possible for me. Not a single jolly obstacle. Might have been married to-morrow morning if I had liked, and sometimes I wish I had been going to act as principal; but it is best as it is."

He was nearing the Rector's residence once again.

" Now with some people," he continued, half aloud, " how different it is. Everything goes wrong with them. Look at poor old Magnus—— The deuce! Why, Mag !"

" I thought you had gone home!"

" I thought you had gone home!"

" I thought I would have a walk first," said Magnus, quietly.

" So did I, old fellow.   But oh, I say!"

" Don't laugh at me, Harry," said the artist, sadly. " It is like saying good-bye. After to-morrow I shall settle down."

" I don't laugh at you, old fellow," said Artingale, taking the other's arm. " It's all right. I might just as well ask you not to laugh at me.   Have a cigar?"

Magnus nodded, the case was produced, and they both lit up, and instead of going straight back east, continued to promenade up and down, and then right round the great block of houses over and over again, for quite an hour, saying very little, but seeming as it were attracted to the place, till coming to the front, for what Artingale vowed should be the last time, he saw a couple of figures apparently leave one of the doors, and go right on towards the other end.

" Somebody late," he said, feeling a kind of interest in the couple that he could not account for.

"Yes," said Magnus, quickly, "very late. Come along."

Artingale involuntarily quickened his steps, and they followed the two figures without a word, seeing them sometimes more, sometimes less, distinctly, according to the position they occupied relative to the lamps.

Why they took so much interest in them was more than they could have explained, for a couple of figures going late at night along a London street is no such very great novelty; but still, they quickened their steps, feeling ready at the slightest hint to have increased the pace to a run.

There seemed no sufficient reason though for such a step, and they continued to walk on fast, till they came to the end of the row of houses; and turning sharply they were just in time to hear the jangling noise of the door of a four-wheeled cab slammed to, then what sounded like a faint wailing cry.

"There's something wrong, I think," said Artingale; but as he spoke the glass was dragged up, the horse started off at a rapid trot, the cab turned into the road by the Park railings, and was gone.

The two friends stood hesitating, and had they been alone, either would have run after the cab. But as they hesitated from a feeling that such a proceeding would have been absurd, the vehicle was driven rapidly away.

"What made you say there was something wrong?" said Magnus at last, in a hoarse voice.

"I don't know, I can't tell: where did those people come from? I hope no one's ill."

"From one of the houses near Mr. Mallow's," said Magnus.

"I think so; I couldn't be sure. Let's walk back."

They hurried back past the series of blank doors, till they were about half way along, when as they reached the Rector's they found that a policeman had just come up, and he made them start by flashing his lantern in their faces.

"Oh, it's you, sir," he said to Artingale. "Were you coming back here?"

"No. Why?"

" Because you left the door open."

" Then there is something wrong, Magnus. Here, let's run after the cab."

" It's half a mile away by now," said the other hoarsely. " You'd better see, constable."

" It's a crack," said the policeman, excitedly, " and the chaps must be in here. Will you gents keep watch while I get help, and put some one on at the other side in the Gardens ?"

" Yes—no—yes," exclaimed Artingale. " I'm afraid some one's ill. We saw two people come away hurriedly and take a cab at the end."

" They wouldn't have took a cab," said the constable. " There's a doctor at the end there close by. We're too late, for a suverin. Or no ; stop. There's something else up. Look here, sir, I've had you hanging about here and on the other side ever since the family has been in town. Now then, who are you ?"

" There is my card, constable," said Artingale, shortly. " You know why I came."

" Yes, sir—my lord, I mean. But why did that big hulking rough chap, like a country gamekeeper, come ? He's been hanging about——"

"Stop!" cried Artingale. "Was it a big black-bearded fellow above six feet high?"

"That's the man, sir. I set him down as from the country house, and after one of the maids."

"When—when did you see him last?" cried Magnus.

"To-night, sir."

"To-night?"

"Yes, m'lord. But while I'm stopping here they may be getting out at the other side and be off."

"I'll watch here," said Artingale.

"Right, sir. I'll soon have some one on at the other side. You, sir, watch at the area"—to Magnus. "If any one comes out and tries to run, you lay hold and stick to 'im. I'll soon be back."

"Quick, then; for heaven's sake, quick!" cried Artingale; and the man went off at a run.

"Let's go after the cab, Harry," cried Magnus, excitedly.

"Let's run after the moon, man. It would be madness. If anything is wrong they are far away by now. But we don't know yet that anything is wrong.   Wait a few minutes. We shall soon find out."

" And meantime ?" panted Magnus.

" We can do nothing but act like men, and remain calm. Go to your post," exclaimed Artingale ; and he spoke in a sharp, decisive way, that showed that the service had missed a good officer.

Five minutes—ten minutes—a quarter of an hour of torture, during which all inside was as still as death. Then as Artingale stood in the open doorway he fancied he heard a slight sound, and as he stood upon the *qui vive*, ready to seize the first man who presented himself, he heard steps outside, and saw that a policeman was coming.

Steps inside, too, and then from the hall a bull's-eye lantern flashed upon him.

" All right, sir," said a familiar voice ; and he saw that it was the first policeman. " The dining-room window was open facing the Park. I come in there. I've got a man watching. That you, sergeant ?"

" Yes. You stop here with this gentleman ;

get out your truncheon, and don't miss 'em, whatever you do. Roberts will be along here directly."

"What are you going to do first?" said Artingale.

"Rout up the butler and one or two more, sir, directly," said the sergeant, opening his lantern; and as they entered the hall he made the light play about the perfectly orderly place, before going softly into the great dining-room.

"Don't quite understand it yet, sir," he said. "The dining-room shutters here had been opened from the inside. Window was open. Seen anything?" he said to some one in the shadow.

"No."

"There's plate enough on that sideboard," continued the sergeant, " to have made a pretty good swag, if it ain't 'lectrer.'"

"No, no, those are all silver. It is a presentation set."

"Then we're in time," whispered the sergeant. "I expect the servants are in it."

A terrible dread was oppressing Artingale,

but he did not speak, only followed the sergeant as he tried the breakfast-room door, to find it fast and the key outside; the library the same.

"All right there," he said softly. "Joe, here. Stand inside and keep your eye on the staircase; we're going below."

The constable at the entrance obeyed his orders, and softly opening a glass door, the sergeant, who seemed quite at home in the geography of the place, led the way down a flight of well-whitened stone steps to the basement, the bright light of his lantern playing upon a long row of bells, and then upon a broad stone passage and several doors.

"Butler's pantry," he whispered, after a good look round. "You stop here, sir."

Artingale stopped short, guarding the foot of the steps, and the sergeant tried the door, to find it fast, but as the handle rattled a man's voice exclaimed, "Who's there?"

"Police! Open quickly."

There was a scuffling noise, then the striking of a match, and a light shone out from three panes of glass above the door. The hurried sound of some one putting on some clothes, and then a peculiar monitory *click-click!*

"Mind what you're at with that pistol," said the sergeant gruffly. "I tell you it's the police. Open the door."

"How do I know it's the police?" said the butler firmly.

"Come and see then, stupid."

"Open the door, Thompson," said Artingale. "I'm here too."

"Oh, is it you, my lord?" said the butler, and he unlocked the door, to be seen in his shirt and trousers, with a cocked pistol in his hand. "I've got the plate here, my lord, and I did not know but what it was a trick. For God's sake, my lord, what's the matter?"

"Don't know yet," said the sergeant. "But the plate's right, you say?"

"Yes; all but the things in the dining-room."

"They're safe too. We found the front door open. Now then, who sleeps down here?"

"Under-butler, footman, and page," said the butler quickly; and taking a chamber candlestick, he led the way to a smaller pantry where the light showed a red-faced boy fast asleep with his mouth open.

" Where are the men ? " said the sergeant laconically ; and the butler led the way to a closed door, which opened into a long stone-paved hall, in the two recesses of which were a couple of turned-up bedsteads, in each of which was a sleeping man, one of whom jumped up, however, as the light fell upon his eyes.

" Get up, James," said the butler. " Have either of you fellows been up to any games ? "

" No, sir. We came to bed before you," was the reply.

" You'd better get up," said the butler.

Then following the sergeant the basement was' searched, and they reascended to the hall.

" I've been all about here," said the sergeant quietly. " They must have meant the jewels and things up-stairs. Next thing is to go up and wake your guv'ner."

" What, alone ? " said the butler blankly.

" Come along, then, and I'll go with you."

"I'll come too, sergeant," said Artingale. "Don't alarm the ladies if you can help it."

And together they mounted the thickly-carpeted stairs.

CHAPTER XIV.

GONE! WHERE?

IF one could but bring oneself to the belief, there is only a slight difference between day and night, and that difference is that in the latter case there is an absence of light—that is all; but, somehow, we people the darkness with untold horrors. We ignore it, of course; we should ridicule the impeachment, but the fact remains the same, that probably nineteen people out of every twenty are afraid of being in the dark—perhaps more so than they were when children.

Possibly we grow more nervous than when we were young, or gas may have had something to do with it; certainly more people seem to burn lights in their bed-rooms than used to be the case before a gas-burner or two had become the regular furniture of a well-ordered bed-room in town.

In our fathers' days, people who were invalids burned long, thin, dismal rushlights in shades, with the candle itself in the middle of a cup of water; or else they had a glass containing so much oil floating on water, and a little wick upon its own raft, sailing about like a miniature floating beacon in the oil. But still these were the exceptions, and a light in a bed-room was an uncommon thing. At the same time, though, it must be allowed that there is something fear-exciting about the dark rooms, and that sounds that are unnoticed in the broad daylight acquire a strange weirdness if heard when all else is still. People have a bad habit of being taken ill in the night; burglars choose "the sma'" hours for breaking into houses; sufferers from indigestion select the darkness for their deeds of evil known as sleep-walking; and the imps attendant on one's muscles prefer two or three o'clock in the so-called morning for putting our legs on that rack known as the cramp. It is perhaps after all excusable then for people to indulge, in moderation. in a little nocturnal alarm ; and it may also. for aught we know, be good for us, and act as a safety-valve escape for a certain amount of bad nerve-force. No doubt Priam was terribly alarmed when his curtains were drawn in the dead of the night— as much so, perhaps, as the mobled queen ; and therefore it was quite excusable for the Rector to answer the summons of the head of his wedding staff of servants in a state of no little excitement.

"Dreadful ! extraordinary ! most strange !" he faltered. "You were passing, Henry, eh ?"

"Yes : Mr. Magnus and I were going by, and we found the policeman had discovered that the door was open."

"Then the place has been rifled," exclaimed the Rector ; "and many of the things are hired," he cried piteously. "Everything will be gone ! What is to be done ?"

"Hush, Mr. Mallow ! we shall alarm the whole house," said Artingale, hastily. "I fancy I saw some one leave the place as we came up. Will you send and see if—if——"

He hesitated, for he saw Magnus with a face like ashes, standing holding on by the balustrade.

"Yes, yes," exclaimed the Rector. "Speak out, please. Do you mean see if all the servants are at home?"

"I don't know—I scarcely know what to say," whispered Artingale, going close up to him. "We want to avoid exposure, sir. Go and knock at Cynthia's door, and send her to see if her sister has been alarmed."

"There is no occasion to frighten her. Let the place below be well searched, and the servants examined."

Just then Mrs. Mallow's voice was heard inquiring what was the matter, and the Rector thrust his head inside the door to tell her that she was not to be alarmed.

"Is any one ill?" said a voice just then, which made Artingale thrill, and he ran to the door from which the voice had come.

"Dress yourself quickly, Cynthy," he whispered, "and go and tell Julie not to be alarmed. We—we are afraid there has been a burglary."

The door closed, and just then the Rector, who had been compelled to go back to his room to quiet Mrs. Mallow's fears, came back.

"I will speak to the young ladies," he said, looking pale and troubled, and going along the landing, he tapped lightly at Julia's door.

"Julia, my dear! Julia!"

He tapped again.

"Julia, my child! Julia!"

Still no answer.

He tapped a little louder, a little louder still — but no answer; and Artingale and Magnus exchanged glances.

"Dear me, it is most embarrassing. How fast she sleeps," said the Rector, looking round apologetically. "Really, gentlemen, I do not think we ought to disturb her."

All the same, urged by a strange feeling of alarm, he tapped again, but still without result; and once more he looked round at the strange group gathered upon the broad landing—the police in great-coats, and lantern-bearing; the butler with his candlestick and pistol ; the two gentlemen in evening dress, with their light overcoats and crush hats in hand.

Just then a door opened, and every one drew back to allow the pretty little vision that burst upon their sight to pass them by.

The figure was that of Cynthia, with her crisp, fair hair lightly tied back, so that it floated down loosely over the loose wide *peignoir* of creamy cashmere trimmed with blue, which formed a costume, as it swept from her in graceful folds, far more becoming than the most ravishing toilet from a Parisian *modiste*. She held a little silver candlestick, with bell glass to shade the light, and as she came forward, looking very composed and firm, though rather pale, Artingale felt for the moment as if he could have emulated Perry-Morton, and fallen down to kiss her pretty little slipper-covered feet.

"Ah, my dear !" exclaimed the Rector, "I am glad you have come. I cannot make Julia hear."

Cynthia darted a quick glance at Artingale, full of dread and dismay, and then without a word she passed on and laid her hand upon the china knob of Julia's door. Then she hesitated for a moment, but only for a moment, before turning the handle and going in, the door swinging to behind her.

Cynthia held her candle above her head and gave one glance round, the light falling on Julia's wedding dress and veil; the wreath was on a table, side by side with the jewels that had been presented to her. Over other chairs and in half-packed trunks were travelling and other costumes, with the endless little signs of preparation for leaving home.

Cynthia gave one glance round her with dilating eyes; ran into the dressing-room and back; looked at the unpressed bed, and then she let fall the candlestick as she sank on her knees uttering a loud cry, and covering her face with her hands.

It was no time for ceremony, and at the cry the Rector rushed in, followed by Artingale, Magnus stopping at the door to keep back the police and the servants, who would have entered too, both the men from below having now joined the group.

As the Rector ran in with Artingale, Cynthia started up once more.

"Oh, papa! oh, Harry!" she cried, piteously, "Julie has gone!"

"Gone!" gasped the Rector. "Gone! Where? Are you mad?"

"Mad? no, papa, but she is. Oh, Harry! I saw that dreadful man to-night outside in the garden, after we had gone to bed; but I thought she would be safe; and now I know it—I am quite sure. Oh, Harry, Harry! what shall we do? He has taken her away!"

CHAPTER XV.

THE BIRD AND THE SERPENT.

UNMISTAKABLY.   There could be no doubt
of the fact; Julia Mallow had fled from her
home that night—half willingly, half forced,
always drawn as it were by the strange influence that the man who had been the evil
genius of her life had exercised over her.

For months past she had fought against it,
and striven to nerve herself to conquer the force
that seemed to master her; but always in vain.
For often, unseen except by her, Jock Morrison was on the watch, turning up where least
expected; and when not present in the flesh,
seemingly always there in spirit, and haunt-
ing her like her shadow.   Again and again he
had come upon her alone, taken her in his

arms, and in his coarse fashion told her that he loved her, and that she should belong to him alone. Nothing, he told her, should keep them apart, for if he could not get her by fair means he would by foul; laughingly showing her the great spring-bladed dagger-knife he carried, and saying that he kept it sharp for any one who got in his way.

Julia trembled at the thought of seeing him; she shuddered and closed her eyes when he appeared before her, and then grew nerveless and weak, fascinated, as it were, like some bird before a serpent; and the scoundrel knew it. He felt the power of his words, and he repeated them to his shivering victim, glorying the while in the power he felt that he exercised over her.

Sometimes she had fancied that she was mastering her fear, but as she overcame that dread, she found, to her horror, that there was another occult influence at work which refused to be overcome; for as in the solitude of her own chamber she strove with it, she found that she was only riveting her chains more stoutly. It was not love for him. No, that was impossible; for she shuddered and shrank from him as from some monster. But, to her horror, she found that her feelings towards the great overmastering ruffian were something near akin. The thoughts of his great muscular figure, his bold bearing, and brown picturesque face were always before her; and even when her own were closed, his fierce black piercing eyes were fixed upon hers, reading her weakness, insisting upon his mastery over her more powerfully even than his words, though they were burned into her memory; and at last, after fighting with all her mind against the current of what she felt to be her fate, she had begun to drift.

Once she had allowed that terrible idea—that it was her fate—to obtain entrance, and she was lost, for it produced a weak submission that stifled every hope. Drift, drift, drift—resigning herself to what she thought was the inevitable. Some day, she told herself, Jock would come and order her to leave home and all she loved, and follow him wheresoever he willed; and she would have to go. He was her master, her fate; and mingled with her horror of him there was that inexplicable fascination that exercised upon her will the power of the mesmerist upon his patient, and she could fight no more. When it would be she knew not, thought not; only she knew that the time would come, and when it did she could no more resist, no more battle with it, than against that other inevitable point that would end her weary life—when the angel of death would overshadow her with his heavy wings, touch her with icy finger, and bid her away.

Always brooding now over these two fixed points in her career—the coming of Jock Morrison and the coming of the end; and so she drifted on. She heard the talk of the wedding that she knew would never be; for if the day did come, and she were taken to the church, she felt that her fate would pluck her from the very altar, or even from her husband's arms.

She knew of the love of James Magnus, and she felt a curious kind of pity for one whom she liked and esteemed; but she closed her eyes with a weary smile as she thought of him, for she knew that she was drifting away, and that even to look at him was to give him pain.

Drifting still when taken to see the talked-of home, asked opinions upon decorations, and taken by father and sister where she was prepared to be decked for the sacrifice. Drifting, too, at party or ball, where she met Perry-Morton, who always seemed to her like some nebulous mist, that was absorbed and died away in the presence of the giant ever filling her imagination.

Go where she would, she felt that she would see him somewhere, though often it was but imagination. Still it kept Jock Morrison always in her mind, and he knew that he was secure of his prize, waiting patiently till she came back from abroad.

At first she had felt a kind of sorrow for Perry-Morton, and wanted to warn him of what her fate would be; but the pity gave place to contempt, the contempt to disgust, the disgust to dread; for she felt that if she warned him he would take steps to assert himself, and if he did, she knew in her heart that her fate, as she called him, would not stop at taking his life.

And so by slow degrees Julia drifted from active opposition into a morbid belief that resistance was vain, nursing her horror in her own racked breast, and waiting for the fulfilment of her fate. As Cynthia had complained, she had grown reticent, and made no confidante of her sister; in fact, there were times, after seeing Morrison, when she felt with a sigh that she should be glad when all was over, and she need think no more. For she was weary of thinking, weary of this keeping up appearances, weary of Perry-Morton, of his sisters, of home, of her own life.

There were times when she looked from her window longingly towards where she knew the long lake lay in the hollow of the Park, and wondered whether it would not be better to flee from the house some evening, go down to the bridge, and throw herself in. She shuddered as she formed the idea; not from dread of death, which would have been like rest to her; but because she felt that she would be only hastening her fate, and that she did fear. For so surely as she left the house to cross the Park, so surely she knew that Jock Morrison would start up from the grass and take her away.

And so it had come to the wedding-eve, and the great burly form had shown itself in the garden. She had seen it early in the evening, and she had felt that it was there hour after hour, till Perry-Morton had left, and she had gone to the window, drawn there in spite of herself. Later on she had obeyed Jock's signals, feeling as if he were speaking to her—telling her that the time had come, and dressing herself in her plainest things, she had sat down and waited by the open window, acting mechanically, till the deep voice came up to where she sat, bidding her come down now.

She felt no emotion, for it was all as if she were in a dream. She obeyed, however, going out on to the landing, after closing her window, to find that all was very silent in the house. Then for a moment she went and kneeled down upon the mat by her sister's door, laid her cheek against it, sighed heavily and kissed the panel that separated them, and slowly descended the stairs, entered the dining-room, and, still as if drawn by her fate, unfastened the shutters and window, which latter was thrown open, and Jock Morrison stepped boldly into the room.

"Good girl!" he said, clasping her in his embrace. "I've got a cab waiting, for you shall ride to-night. Didn't you think it was time I came?"

She did not answer, but acted still like one in a dream, as he watched from the door, withdrawing more than once with a muttered oath as Artingale and Magnus kept parading about the place.

He was about to start again and again, but he always seemed to hesitate till their steps were heard once more, when he would close the door and stand listening, with the trembling girl clasped tightly in his arms.

At last he seemed to be satisfied that the ground was clear, and with a smile of triumph on his lip he stepped out, drawing Julia after him; but as he reached the pavement he heard the steps of the two gentlemen once more, and uttering a fierce oath he hurried his prize along faster and faster, as he felt that their evasion had been seen.

"Quicker, my lass, quicker!" he said, gruffly; and she had to obey him. But she was growing faint. She held up, though, till she reached the cab, into which he hurried her. And now for the first time the reality of her position seemed to force itself upon her, and she started up with a wild cry.

Too late! With one hand he thrust her back into the seat as with the other he drew up the window, and her next feeble cry was drowned by the noise of the jangling panes.

In his agony of grief and horror the Rector could hardly believe in the possibility of that which Artingale reluctantly told; for when he appealed to his child he could not get a word from her, but hysterical cries for her sister, whom she accused herself of having neglected and allowed to go.

It was impossible, the Rector declared, and after a long discussion he insisted upon the matter being kept quiet, refusing to take any steps in the way of pursuit till he had seen his son.

It would all come right, he was sure, he said; and finding that nothing could be done, Artingale left the house, after hearing from the doctor, who had been sent for, that he need be under no apprehension concerning Cynthia.

"What next?" he said to Magnus.

"To find her," said the artist, "wherever she is, and to bring her back—poor lost lamb! Oh, Harry, they have driven the poor girl mad!"

"I'm with you, Magnus," said Artingale, "to the end. Come on; we have lost much valuable time, but I could not stir till I saw what her father intended to do."

He hailed a cab.

"Scotland Yard!" he shouted, and the man drove on. "If it costs me all I've got I'll have her back. I look upon her as a sister. Poor girl! poor girl! she must have been mad indeed."

"Harry," whispered Magnus, "what are you going to do?" and his voice sounded hoarse and strange.

"Put the best dogs to be had upon the trail to run them down."

"And then?"

"Get the scoundrel transported for life. And you?"

"I'm going with you to-night, or this morning, or whatever it is; to-morrow I'm going to buy a pistol."

"And blow out your brains?" cried Artingale. "Bah! what's the use of that?"

"No," said Magnus, turning his haggard face to his friend, "to shoot him as I would a rabid dog."

"And be put on your trial for murder. No; my plan's best."

"Your plan!" said Magnus, fiercely. "What can you do? You forget the circumstances of the case. Before we can reach them the scoundrel will have married her. You cannot touch him."

Artingale ground his teeth as he seemed to realize the truth of what was said. Then, turning, he urged the man on to greater speed.

All was quiet and orderly in the great office at Whitehall, and a quiet, thoughtful official heard their business, raised his eyebrows a little, and then made a few notes.

"You will keep the matter as quiet as possible," said Artingale, "for the sake of the young lady's family; but at all costs she must be brought back."

"We'll soon find the scoundrel, my lord; but from your description he is not a London man."

"London, no; he is one of those scoundrels who live more by poaching than anything."

"All right, sir. I'll take your address—and yours, sir. Can I find you here—at what time?"

"Time!" cried Artingale: "I have no time but for this affair. I'll stay here with you and your men—live here—sleep here. Damme, I'll join the force if it will help to bring the poor child back. It is horribly bad! She was to have been married this morning."

"All that can be done, sir, shall be done,"

said the officer, quietly. "And now, gentlemen, if you'll take my advice you'll go home
and have a good sleep."

"What!" cried Artingale. "Go and sleep?
No, I want to be at work."

"Exactly, sir; then go and have a rest,
and be ready for when I want you. If you
stop here you can do no good—only harm,
by hindering me."

"But, damn it all!" cried Artingale,
furiously, "you take it so coolly."

"The only way to win, sir—my lord, I
mean. But we are wasting time. By now
I should have had the telegraph at work, and
the description flying to every station in
London."

"In God's name, then, go on," cried Artingale, "take no notice of us, only let us
stay."

The officer nodded, and in an incredibly
short space of time it was known all over
London and the districts round of the elope-
ment or abduction, and a couple of the keenest
officers were at work to track the fugitives
down.

It took some time; but a clever net was drawn all over London. The early morning trains were watched, the yards where the night cabs were housed were visited; the various common lodging-houses had calls, and every effort was made to trace Jock Morrison, and had he been a known London bird the probabilities are that the police would have placed their hands upon him; but they had to deal with a man whose life had been one of practised cunning, and he had so made his plans that the police were at fault.

They found the cabman in a very short time, and he testified to having driven the great fellow and the lady with him to Charing Cross.

That was all.

The net spread over London missing that which it was intended to catch, its meshes were lessened, and it was stretched out wider, and from every police-station in the country, and in every provincial town, the description of the fugitives went forth; but still they were not found. So cleverly had the scoundrel made his plans that no tidings whatever were obtained, and by degrees the pursuit waxed less hot. First one and then another *cause célèbre* took the attention of the police. Then Artingale grew less keen, for the months were gliding by, and he had devoted himself heart and soul to the cause for long enough without result.

Then more months passed, and still no news. The strange disappearance of Julia Mallow became almost historical, and it was only revived a little as a topic of conversation, when it was announced that Mr. Perry-Morton had returned with his sisters from their long sojourn in Venice, and soon after it was rumoured in paragraphs that the talented leader of a certain clique was about to lead to the altar the daughter of a most distinguished member of the artistic world.

Luke Ross had been consulted by Magnus and Lord Artingale, and had helped them to the best of his power, counselling the enlistment of Tom Morrison and his wife upon their side; but he could do no more, and the matter was pushed from his mind by the hard study and work upon which he was engaged, till he read in the morning papers the announcement of Cynthia's marriage to Lord Artingale, quite two years after Julia's disappearance, the Mallows having again been a long time abroad.

Then, saving to a few, Julia was as one that is dead.

CHAPTER XVI.

A MEETING—AND PARTING.

THREE years passed away, and Julia's disappearance remained a mystery to all, and it was calmly put away upon the dusty shelves of the past—by all save one.

Father had mourned for her, and time had somewhat assuaged his grief; mother had wept in silence upon her weary couch; sister talked less often now of 'poor Julia'; brother, when he was seen, never mentioned her name. The whole matter had grown misty and pale in the distance of the bygone to all save James Magnus, and from that night he had never rested. Detectives had grown cold; other affairs had taken their attention; but nothing had checked the cold, stern, haggard man whose one aim in life now was to stand face to face with the ruffian who had made his life a wreck. Had Julia married Perry-Morton, he would have borne it in silence; but this was an outrage to his feelings that he could not bear, and taking sketching materials as an excuse, he had started off to find them, though he rarely put brush to paper now, for he was incessant in his searchings, and every likely nook and corner in London and the great cities was visited by him in turn.

Now he was wandering in the country, having had news that seemed to promise success; now away off to some out-of-the-way spot in the New Forest, or Herefordshire, where gipsies made their home; always on the scent, but never successful. He had tracked out scores of burly ruffians, but they were none of them the man he thought to meet.

Back again in London in the east, in the lowest purlieus of the south, in common lodging-houses, on waste grounds where caravans were drawn up for the winter; off to race-courses and fairs, and great markets where such men as Jock Morrison were to be found, but always in vain.

Once he heard of him, as he thought, at Horncastle, at another time at Newmarket, and again on Epsom Downs, but it was always some great idle ruffian bearing a slight resemblance to Jock Morrison, never the man himself.

And in all those solitary wanderings, James Magnus carried the pistol he had bought, and practised with it in his lonely walks. Hundreds upon hundreds of times those chambers were discharged, his marks being trees, finger-posts, saplings rising out of hedges; and though the artist seemed day by day to grow thin, careworn, and weak, his nerves were as if of steel, and each bullet flew upon its course with unerring aim.

"The law cannot touch him," he muttered, with a strange smile; "perhaps a bullet can."

It was on a bright afternoon in May that, seeing no beauty in the verdant spring and the return of sunny days, James Magnus, heartsick and worn out, crawled back to his chambers to find Burgess anxiously expecting him, for he had been away longer than was his wont.

"Oh, I am glad to see you back, sir," he said. "Set down, sir, and let me take off your dusty boots. You look worn out. Lord Harry has been here—not an hour ago."

A faint smile came upon the face of Magnus, as he heard the name of his friend, and taking up the card he rose to go.

"Going, sir, so soon?" exclaimed his man.

"Only to see Lord Artingale," said Magnus, wearily. "I'll soon be back."

On reaching his friend's house in Lowndes-square, the servant told him that his lordship had gone into the Park with her ladyship. They were in the open carriage; and wondering at his own weariness, Magnus followed, unconsciously walking straight to the very spot where, what seemed a lifetime back, he and Artingale had leaned over the rail, and first seen poor Julia's fate.

He did not recall the fact at first, but stood watching the carriages, thinking how much he would like to meet his old friend; and his face lit up with a smile that had been a stranger to it of late.

For a long time it seemed as if his journey

had been in vain, and he was listlessly scanning the long lines of vehicles, when suddenly he heard his name uttered, and a carriage was drawn up close to the rails, with Artingale and Cynthia therein, both looking, if not so young, as bright and happy as ever.

"My dear old fellow," cried Artingale, grasping his friend's hand, as Cynthia possessed herself of the other, "I can't tell you how glad I am to see you. But jump in, and we'll go home at once. We'll have such a dinner, and those dining-room curtains shall be incensed, and no mistake, to-night."

"No, no, not now," said Magnus; and in spite of all his friend's pressure he declined.

"Then I shall come with you," cried Artingale. "Cynthy, may I go?"

"I suppose you must," she said merrily. "Mr. Magnus, you are the only gentleman to whom I would give him up."

Then there was a pleasant chat for a time, the carriage drove on, and Artingale and his friend were left standing by the Park rails.

"Not one word," said Magnus to himself; "Julia is indeed dead."

"Why, Mag, old man, this is the very spot where——"

"Hush! Look!" cried Magnus, grasping his friend's arm. "God, I thank Thee. At last—at last!"

Artingale followed the direction of his eyes, and started, for there, on the other side of the drive, was the great picturesque ruffian, slowly sauntering along, quite unchanged, and with the same defiant air.

Artingale restrained his friend, who was about to leap over the railings.

"No, no," he whispered, "let's follow him, and see where he goes. We shall find her then."

It was a slow task, for Jock Morrison went first out on to the grass and lay down for an hour, but the watchers did not quit their post for a moment, but tracked him when he rose, step by step, and along the great highway due east, till he turned up Gray's-inn-lane, and then up one of the narrow courts.

It was as ill-favoured and vile as any there, and for the moment Magnus thought he had missed his man, but as, in spite of the scowling looks around, he hurried down the court, a heavy step on one of the staircases acted as his guide; and, closely followed by Artingale, he bounded up to the second landing, which he reached just as a door was slammed to, and he turned a countenance upon his friend that made him shudder.

"At last, Harry," he said in a low whisper. "At last! God of heaven, how I have prayed for this time !"

"Stop," cried Artingale, excitedly; "you shall not go in. Give me that pistol, Magnus. You shall not go."

He clung to his friend's arm, but Magnus threw him off.

That there was no mistake was evident, for from beyond the filthy paintless door came the hoarse bullying tones of the fellow's voice, and, unable to contain himself longer, Magnus dashed open the door, and stepped in.

He was greeted by a volley of oaths, and the great ruffian started up from a bed upon the floor where he had evidently thrown himself down, and as he did so, with a face like ashes and his teeth set, Magnus covered him with his pistol.

Artingale was in the doorway, and saw it all, but stood paralyzed at his friend's act. But another moment, and the bullet would have sped upon its deadly errand, when, with a cry, a woman threw herself between them, placing herself with her back against Jock's breast, and her arms thrown up to screen his face, as, with flaming eyes, she faced the intruders upon her home.

"Stand aside, Ju, I'm not afraid of his barker," roared the great ruffian, with a blasphemy; but the woman clung to him and held him back as the pistol dropped upon the floor, and Magnus staggered against his friend.

The recognition was mutual, but the woman's face remained unchanged. It was filled with the passionate desire to protect the ruffian who treated her a little worse than he would have treated his dog; and as he read the history of her life in what he saw, Artingale stood speechless for a few moments, while Jock swung his defender on one side, strode forward quickly, and picking up the pistol, put it in his pocket.

"Julia," exclaimed Artingale, recovering

himself and advancing, "do you not know me?"

She looked at him fixedly for a few moments. Her face began to quiver, and her hand was slightly raised to take the one he extended; but she became rigid directly after, and turned away to cling to Jock Morrison, who, with his hands in his pockets, looked mockingly on.

"No," she said, in a sharp, harsh voice, as changed as was her thin, worn, piteous face from that Artingale had known in better days. "No," she said, "I do not know you; the Julia you knew is dead."

"Well," said the great fellow, roughly, "have you any more to say to my wife? Because if not, go."

Artingale felt like one in a dream, as he fell back, and the door slammed to; then slowly descending, careless of the curious eyes and scowling looks directed at them, he joined his friend, and they went back to the studio, where Magnus threw himself wearily down and closed his eyes.

"But I must do something," exclaimed

Artingale ; and, rushing out, he had himself driven to Great Scotland-yard.

"What can you do, my lord?" said the officer he saw. "From what you say, the fellow has married her, and we can't undo that. I'll take what steps you like, my lord, but——"

But! There was a volume in that one word, for when afterwards effort after effort was made to win the wanderer back by father, mother, sister, all was in vain. She had spoken truly. The Julia whom Harry Artingale had known was dead.

It was close upon twelve that same night that, sick at heart, Artingale returned to his friend's chambers, to find that Burgess had been busy preparing supper, feeling sure that he would return.

"Where is your master?" said Artingale.

"He said he would go and lie down, sir, till you came. He thought you would be sure to come back to-night. But oh, my lord—oh sir," cried the poor fellow piteously, "can't you do something to make poor master what he was? This is weary work indeed!"

"I don't know, Burgess. I can't say. I'll try, but I hope he will be better now."

"I hope and pray he may, sir," said the man, fervently; and Artingale went on into the bed-room, to see that his friend had placed Julia's picture on the easel at the farther side of the bed in full sight from where he.lay; and as the young man's eyes lighted upon the prostrate figure, he uttered a cry which brought in the man.

"Quick, Burgess, quick! The nearest doctor."

A fruitless errand: James Magnus, after his long and weary pilgrimage, was resting peacefully where there is no dreaming of revenge.

Of a broken heart! So it was said, for the secret was well kept. There are men who dare to make the rush headlong from this world.

BOOK III.—THE BARRISTER'S DAY.

CHAPTER I.

IN CHAMBERS.

"With a rum-tum, tum-tum, tiddy-iddy tum, tiddy-rum-tum, tiddy-iddy bang!"

This was sung in a low-pitched, not unmusical voice, by a stunted, thickly-set lad of seventeen or eighteen, being his version of the well-known "March of the British Grenadiers"; and as he puffed forth the air in imitation of a wind instrument, the musical youth paraded the well-furnished office he occupied, with an enormous ebony ruler over his shoulder, held sword-fashion, and the stove poker in his left hand carried like a scabbard.

He was so far on the alert that he kept one eye upon a green baize-covered inner door, evidently leading into a private room, but not sufficiently watchful to see that another door had been opened, for as he got through a second strain of the march he called, softly, in imitation of a commanding officer, "Halt!—right about face. Band to the front!" Then his jaw dropped, and he made a bound to his desk.

The reason of this change was that a stern, dry-looking, well-dressed man stood there, with an umbrella in one hand, 'a blue bag in the other, and he did not smile, but showed his teeth slightly, as he saw the lad's confusion.

"Drilling, eh?" he said, shutting the door close behind him. "Going to join the army?"

"No, sir," said the boy, smartly.

"Of course not," said the visitor. "Much too short."

"Please, sir, I can't help that," said the boy, whose face was now scarlet; "and I shall grow."

"Only wiser, boy," said the visitor, "not taller. Wiser; and then you won't go and be shot at for a few pennies a day. Mr. Ross in?"

"Don't know, sir. I'll see," said the boy.

" Yes, you do know," snarled the visitor ; " and he is in, or else you wouldn't have gone about on tiptoe. Take in my card."

" Mr. Swift, Cripple and Swift," read the boy.

" Yes, and be quick. Time's money, boy."

" Yes, sir. Take a chair, sir," said the lad, whose martial ardour had cooled into business ; and he opened the baize door, let it close behind him, and knocked at the panel of an inner door, the knock sounding muffled and distant to the visitor.

" Come in !"

The boy entered a handsomely-furnished room, in the middle of whose Turkey carpet was a large, well-drawered writing-table, covered with papers tied up in red and green tape. On one side was a handsome. polished wardrobe, half open. displaying. hanging from pegs. a couple of barrister's gowns. looking in the dim interior like a couple of old-fashioned clergymen hung up to dry, or for some other reason.

In another polished-wood cupboard, with glass doors partly covered with blinds, were apparently a couple of stuffed barristers in their wigs, gazing mournfully through the glass at the opening door of the office, till a second inspection showed them to be wig-blocks, with their legal horsehair burdens grey and stiff.

Cases full of thick volumes, a couple of busts of famous judges in their wigs, and here and there an almanack, a pale blue sheet of paper, printed with the dates of various judges' circuits, and, lastly, a tall oaken case full of pigeon-holes stuffed to overflowing with legal papers, formed the surroundings of him who said "Come in."

The speaker was in a dressing-gown and slippers, seated at the writing-table, with his head resting upon his hands, evidently study-ing intently the contents of certain sheets of paper, closely written in a clear round hand, but with a broad margin, whereon from time to time the reader made notes, by means of a gold pencil-case.

His face was bent so low that nothing but the broad forehead was visible when he set one hand at liberty to write; but it could

he seen that this broad, open brow was lined
by study, and the dark hair was cut off closely
to the reader's head.

He did not look up when the boy entered,
but said, in a quick, decided voice—

"Well, Dick?"

"Gentleman to see you, sir," said the boy;
and he placed a card upon the writing-table,
at which card the reader glanced, but without
changing his position.

"H'm, Mr. Swift," he said. "Show him in."

The visitor needed scarcely any showing, for
as the boy went back he was ready to step in
at once, and his stern, harsh, rather unpleasant
face seemed to wear a satisfied air as he took
all in at a glance.

"Good morning, Mr. Ross," he said, as the
reader rose and showed the face of Luke Ross,
twelve years older, and pale and thin, but with
his dark eyes, rather deeply set, now full of
vigorous intelligence, as he seemed to look his
visitor through and through, and motioned
him to a seat with a wave of a thin, delicate
white hand, upon which shone a heavy unorna-
mented signet ring.

"I think you know our name, Mr. Ross," said the visitor, with an air of self-satisfaction, as he laid his blue bag across his knees.

"Perfectly well, Mr. Swift," said Ross, quietly. "I was against you in that shipping case last week."

"Yes, sir, you were," said the visitor, with a smile that looked like a snarl; "and you beat us, sir—beat Philliman—and that's why I have come."

"Mr. Philliman worked very hard for your client, Mr. Swift," said Luke, quietly. "I presume that you bear no malice?" he added, with a smile.

"Malice, sir—malice, Mr. Ross? Ha, ha, ha! That's very good, sir—uncommonly good. I'll tell Cripple as soon as I return."

"I know you'll excuse me, Mr. Swift," said the young barrister, glancing at his watch, "if I tell you that my time is very much occupied."

"Of course! To be sure. Yes, my dear sir," said the visitor, busily opening his blue bag. "I know it is. But as it was our first affair with you, I thought I would come on myself instead of sending our clerk. There, sir," he exclaimed, drawing out a folded packet of papers, tied up with tape, "I have come to show you how we bear malice, sir—our first brief."

As he spoke he handed the papers to Luke Ross with the triumphant smile of one who is conferring a great favour, and then, throwing himself back in his chair, he looked quite disappointed as the barrister just glanced at the endorsement on the brief, which, among other words, bore certain hieroglyphics in a crabbed hand—"15 *gs.*"

"I am sorry to have troubled you to come. Mr. Swift," said Luke, in a quiet, grave voice, that was very impressive, and, though low, seemed to fill the room, "but I really must decline."

"Decline!" exclaimed the solicitor, flushing. "Do you know, Mr. Ross, that this may mean an enormous number of briefs from our firm, sir—a very fortune?"

Luke bowed.

"You are a young man, Mr. Ross—excuse me for saying so, sir—just making a name in your profession. Do I understand you aright, sir? Our firm, sir, stands high."

"Perfectly aright, Mr. Swift," replied Luke, in a voice that quite seemed to silence the solicitor, who refreshed himself with a hastily-taken pinch of snuff, and shut the lid of his box with a loud snap. "I know your firm well, sir; but, as you are aware," he added, with a grave smile, "there are limits to even an enterprising barrister's powers, and the profession has been kind enough to give me more than I care to undertake."

"Ah, exactly, sir—of course—yes," said Mr. Swift, smiling, and nodding his head. "Exactly so, my dear sir. Will you allow me?"

Luke bowed, and before he had quite realized his visitor's intentions, he had caught up a quill pen, and, rapidly dipping it, altered the fifteen on the back of the brief with a couple of touches into twenty-five, blotted it, and handed it to the young barrister, who raised his hand not to take the brief, but to decline.

"I am sorry, Mr. Swift," he said, "but I have sent back a couple of briefs this morning marked preciseyl as you have endorsed that. I am obliged to decline. Try Mr. Norris, or Mr. Henrich, on this staircase. I am sure they will be glad to accept the brief."

The solicitor stared in astonishment, took out his snuff-box, put it back again, and then exclaimed sharply—

" But I want *you*, sir, YOU."

" Then," said Luke, smiling, " I am afraid you will have to double the fee upon the brief, Mr. Swift. So much work has come to me of late, that I have been compelled to make that my fee."

· " And with a refresher, sir?" said the solicitor, dropping the patronizing air for one of increased respect.

" And with a refresher, sir," replied the young barrister.

Mr. Swift glanced from him to the brief he had been studying and back.

" Why, you are not in Regina *versus* Finlayson, sir?" he said. " Morley and Shorter told me that they had given the brief to some one, endorsed fifty."

" I am the humble individual, Mr. Swift,"

said Luke, who in his calm, grave way seemed to be amused.

Without another word the solicitor snatched up the quill, dipped it, and dashing out the twenty-five guineas, rapidly wrote above it "50 *gs.*"

"There, sir," he said, blotting it with a bang upon the writing-table, "we must have you, sir. We want to have you, Mr. Ross. You will take this for us—it's for the prosecution, sir,—a most important case. It is, really, sir."

"It is astonishing how often the case is most important in the eyes of the firm of solicitors, and how very ordinary it turns out, Mr. Swift, when it comes into court. But there, Mr. Swift, I'll do my best for your client," and he rose.

The solicitor took the hint, and picked up his hat and blue bag.

"Thank you, Mr. Ross; thank you, sir. I am very, very glad. Our first brief, Mr. Ross. The first, sir, of many. Good morning."

He shook hands with a look of the most profound veneration for the eminent young legal light, whose brilliancy was beginning to be discussed a good deal, both in and out of court.

"Good morning, Mr. Swift," said Luke. "I'll try and get you a verdict."

"You will, sir; I'm sure you will," said the solicitor, bowing as he reached the door, and then hurrying back. "One moment, Mr. Ross—a word from an old limb of the law, sir. You are a young man, and not above listening to advice."

"Certainly not," said Luke, smiling, "if it be good."

"'Tis good, sir. Take it. Do away with that boy, and have a quiet, elderly clerk, sir. Gives dignity to your office. Good morning."

He nodded this time, and shut the door after him, carefully opened the baize portal, and passed through that, to change his whole aspect as he found a very tall, thin, cadaverous-looking man, in glossy black, and with a heavy gold eye-glass swinging outside his buttoned-up surtout.

The countenance of the tall, thin man

changed a little, too; but they shook hands warmly.

"Won't do, Hampton, if you've come about the Esdaile case," he said.

"Never you mind what I've come about," said the tall man, with asperity.

"Oh, I don't, my dear sir, for we've got Ross for the prosecution."

"Con——— Tut, tut, tut. Oh, hang it, Swift, this is too bad."

"Ha, ha, ha!" laughed the solicitor.

"But, look here, honour bright?"

"Honour bright, my dear sir. Go and ask him."

"I'll take your word, Swift. Give me a pinch of snuff. What, have you endorsed the brief, eh?"

The solicitor whispered.

"Have you, though? Well, I should have done the same. It will be silk one of these days."

"Safe, sir, safe," said the other; and they went out together, just as a cab stopped at the end of the narrow lane, and, looking very thin and old, and dry, but bright and active still, old Michael Ross stepped out ; and then, with a very shabby, long old carpet bag in one hand, and a baggy green umbrella, with staghorn handle, in the other, trotted down the incline into the Temple till he reached the staircase, at the foot of which, on one of the door-posts, was painted a column of names.

"Hah !" said the old man, smiling, as he set down his bag, and balanced a clumsy pair of glasses on his nose, holding them up with one hand. "This is it. Number nine. Ground floor, Mr. Sergeant Towle ; Mr. Barnard, Q.C. First floor, Mr. Ross."

"Hah !" he muttered, with a chuckle, "first floor, Mr. Ross. I wonder whether he's at home.

"No," he ejaculated. "That's wrong. Should be, ' I wonder whether he's in court.' "

The old man stopped short in the entry, with the door leading to Mr. Sergeant Towle's chambers before, and that leading to the chambers of Mr. Barnard, Q.C., behind, and drew forth his washed-out and faded red cotton handkerchief.

" I wonder whether he'll be glad to see me," he said. "I'm only a shabby-looking old fellow, and I dare say I've brought the smell of the tan-pits with me; and they tell me my son is getting to be quite a famous lawyer—quite the gentleman, too. Ah, it's a great change—a great change. And I didn't tell him I was coming; and p'raps it isn't right to take him so by surprise. He mightn't like it."

The old man rubbed his damp fingers on his handkerchief, and looked about him in a troubled, helpless way.

"I feel always so mazed-like in this noisy London," he said, weakly; "and if he was hurt about my coming it would about break my heart, that it would."

The handkerchief was on its way up to his eyes, where the weak tears were gathering, when there was the sound of voices in the chambers of Mr. Sergeant Towle, and, snatching up his bag, the old man trotted, pretty nimbly, up the stone stairs to the first floor, where, upon the pale drab door, there was the legend, "Mr. Ross."

"Mr. Ross," said the old man, chuckling to himself. "Mr. Ross. That's my son. God bless him! My son; and I'd have given a hundred golden pounds if my dear old wife had been alive, and could have stood here and seen his name writ large and famous on a door in London town like that."

He stood admiring it for some minutes, and then hesitated, as if overcome by the importance of his son; but at last he raised the big umbrella, and tapped gently with the staghorn beak.

It was a very modest knock, and it was not answered, so at the end of five minutes he knocked again.

This time Mr. Richard Dixie—Dicky Dix, as he was familiarly called—verified the words of Mr. Swift, the solicitor (Cripple and Swift, of Gresham-street), by staring hard at the shabby-looking little old man and his bag, and then coming a little way out to stare at the doorpost, to the surprise of old Ross.

"It ain't broke," said the boy.

"What isn't broke, sir?" said the old man, humbly.

That 'sir' was like so much nerve to one who did not need it; and, turning sharply to

the old man, he gave another glance at the
shabby bag.

"Then what do you want to come a banging
at the door with your old umbrelly for?"

"I didn't see the bell, sir," said the old
man, humbly. "Is—is your master in?"

"Got anything to sell?" said the boy,
sharply.

"To sell, sir? Yes; a good deal. The
market's been very bad lately. Is your master,
Mr. Ross, in?"

"No, he ain't," said the boy, sharply.
"Don't want any. Take your bag somewhere
else. We gets ours at the stationer's."

The old man stood aghast, for the boy gave
his bag a kick and shut the door to sharply,
without another word.

"He's a quick, sharp boy," said the old
man; "very impudent though. A regular
London boy; and Luke's out. Well, well,
well, I've come a long way to see him, and
I can wait," and without another word, the old
man seated himself patiently at the foot of
the next flight of stairs, placing his bag beside
him, and his green umbrella across his knees.

CHAPTER II.

IN TROUBLE.

"Sage? What—down-stairs?" cried Mrs. Portlock. "Don't say they're in trouble again, Joseph."

"Why not?" said the Churchwarden, slowly. "Come along down, and make the poor girl some warm tea. She's been travelling all night, and has brought the two little ones with her."

"I'll be down directly," said Mrs. Portlock; "but what is the matter?"

"Trouble, trouble, trouble," said the Churchwarden, slowly. "Hang the laws. I'd give something if I could take her away from him, and keep her at home, children and all. It would come a deal cheaper, old lady."

"Oh, but you are too hard on him, Joseph, indeed you are. Cyril is very, very fond of her and his children."

"Bah! I never knew him fond of anything but himself, and what money he could get."

"There, if you are in that kind of temper, Joseph, it is of no use for me to speak to you. I'll be down directly; but won't Sage come up?"

"No, I've made her lie down on the sofa by the fire. She's worn out, and the little ones are fast asleep. I've told the girls to hurry on the breakfast."

"But how foolish of her to travel in the night. How did they come from the station?"

"A man brought them in a cart. Poor things! they are half perished."

"Dear, dear, dear, dear me," said Mrs. Portlock, hastily dressing. "What troubles there are in this world."

"Yes, if people make 'em."

"But what is wrong with Cyril?"

"Oh, nothing particular," said the Church-warden, bitterly, "only he's in trouble again."

"In trouble?"

"Yes, in trouble. Don't shout about it and frighten the poor girl more."

"But what does it mean?"

"Oh, some trouble over old Walker's affairs. Sage says she is sure he is innocent. Heaven knows I hope he is."

"But what made her come down?"

"What made her come down, old lady? Why, what was the poor wench to do, a woman with a couple of little children? There, it seems a sin to say so, but it's a blessing the others died."

"Oh, for shame, Joseph!" cried Mrs. Portlock, whose trembling old fingers were in great trouble over various strings.

"I don't care," said the Churchwarden, whose hair was white now, but who looked as sturdy and well as ever; "I wish she had never seen the scoundrel."

"Joseph, if you talk like that, you'll break the poor girl's heart."

"I'm not going to talk to her like that, but I suppose I may to you. Here have they been married close upon twelve years, and what have they been but twelve years of misery?"

"There has been a deal of trouble certainly," sighed Mrs. Portlock. "What time is it now?"

"Half-past six. Make haste. He was held to be all that was steady and right at that Government appointment, and six months after his marriage they kicked him out."

"But Sage always said, dear, that they behaved very ill to Cyril."

"Of course she did, and she believed it, poor lass; but if half that I heard of him was true, I'd have kicked him out at the end of three months instead of six."

"It's very, very shocking," sighed Mrs. Portlock, getting something in a knot.

"Then he gets his mother's money; poor soul, she'd have sold herself for that boy."

"Yes; she's very, very fond of him."

"There was enough for them to have lived in comfort to the end of their days, if he hadn't bet and squandered the property all away."

"I'm afraid he was a little reckless," sighed Mrs. Portlock.

"Reckless? He was mad. Then, when it

was gone, it was money, money, money : never a month passing but there was a letter from poor Sage, begging for money."

"But she couldn't help it, dear."

"Think I don't know that," cried the Churchwarden, striding to and fro. "He forced her to write, of course; and we sent it, but not for him. If it hadn't been for her and the bairns, not a penny of my hard savings would he ever have seen."

"But he has been better lately."

"Better? Ha, ha, ha! So it seems. Wait till we know all. Five thousand pounds gone in that wine merchant's business."

"Well, but, Joseph, dear, you would have left it to them after we were dead. Wasn't it better to give it to them at once?"

"Yes, if it was for their good," said the Churchwarden. "What is it? Four years ago, and Mallow said, 'No,'—I remember his words as well as if it were only yesterday— 'No,' he said, 'I think we've done enough. My wife's money has all gone to him, and I will not impoverish myself further. I think it is your turn, now.'"

"Well, Joseph," said Mrs. Portlock, who had nearly arrived at the stage of dressing that calls for a cap, "that was only fair."

"Oh, yes, it was fair enough; and I wouldn't have grudged it if Cyril had been like other men. Five thousand pounds hard savings I paid down that he might go into partnership with old Walker in that wine trade."

"Well, and I'm sure they seem to have done well for some time, Joseph ; and see what a nice present of wine Cyril sent you every Christmas. Yes, for five Christmas presents, Joseph."

"Every one of which cost me a thousand pounds, old lady, and the interest. Dear presents—dear presents."

"But he was getting on well, Joseph, and he seemed so steady ; and I'm sure he was very fond of Sage."

"Fond of Sage!" cried the old farmer, bitterly. "Don't tell me. How can a man be fond of his wife when he spends every penny he can get on himself, and then turns the woman he swore to protect into a begging-letter writer?"

"But what does it all mean? Only the other day, dear," said Mrs. Portlock, whose hands trembled, and who seemed sadly agitated, "we heard that old Mr. Walker had died, and I thought it meant that now Cyril would have the business all to himself."

"Yes, and he has had it all to himself," said the Churchwarden, bitterly. "But come down, and speak gently to her, poor darling. Let's do all we can to make the best of things."

The Churchwarden had let the angry excitement escape in the presence of his wife, and there was a notable change in his manner as he softly followed her down into the old parlour, where a bonny fire was blazing, and Sage Mallow had changed her position to the easy-chair, so that her little ones might enjoy the comfort of the broad old sofa, drawn, as it was, before the glow.

They were fast asleep, the two pretty little girls, with their tangled hair, in a close embrace, and warmly covered with a great rug, while their mother lay back in the chair, looking twenty years older than on the day she accompanied Cyril Mallow to the church.

Her face was pinched and pale, and about her lips there was that strange compression that tells of suffering, weariness, and an aching heart.

A sigh broke involuntarily from the Church-warden's breast, as with tender solicitude he went down on one knee, and drew a shawl over the sleeping mother's arms.

It was softly done, but Sage started into wakefulness, and then, seeing who was there, her dilate and frightened eyes softened with tears as she threw her arms round his neck, and hid her face in his breast, sobbing hysterically, but in a low, weary way.

"Oh, uncle, uncle!"

"My poor bairn, my dear bairn," he whispered, drawing her closer to his breast, and softly caressing her hair. "There, there, there, don't cry, don't cry. As long as there's a roof at Kilby, and we're alive, there's a home for you, my darling, and the little ones. So come, come, come, cheer up!"

"But my husband," she said, wildly, as she looked up, and, for the first time, saw that Mrs. Portlock was present. "Oh, auntie, auntie," she wailed, almost in a whisper, as she cast an anxious glance at the sleeping children, "I'm in such trouble, and such grief. What shall I do?"

She quitted her uncle's embrace now, to lay her head, with the weariness of a sick child, upon the old lady's breast.

"There, there," whispered her aunt, with all the sharp jerkiness of manner gone. "Cheer up a bit, and we'll see what's to be done. You did quite right to come down. Uncle and I will take care of you and the bairns."

"But I must go back directly," said Sage, sitting up and smoothing her hair. "I came down to ask uncle and Mr. Mallow to help us, but Mr. Mallow is so angry with Cyril that I am almost afraid to go."

"Oh, I'll go and have a talk to him, my darling," said the Churchwarden; "and we'll see if we can't set things a bit right. Ah, that's better," he cried, as one of the maids entered with a hot cup of tea. "There, my dear, drink that. Don't wait, Anne."

The girl, who was staring open-mouthed, left the room, and, after some persuasion, Sage drank the tea.

"I want to tell you, uncle," she cried, after holding her hands for a few moments to her temples, as if her head was confused, and her thoughts wandering away. "I want to tell you all, but I seem to be hearing the rattle of the train in my head, and jolting over the road in that cart, with the children crying with the cold."

"But they are fast asleep, and comfortable now, my girl," said the Churchwarden, soothingly. "Suppose you have a nap, and tell us all your trouble later on."

"No, no," she cried, "I must tell you now, for I want to get back to Cyril."

She stared about so wildly that the Churchwarden and his wife exchanged glances.

"Is Cyril at home, then?" said Portlock, as if to help her regain the current of her thoughts.

"Home?" she cried. "No: we have no home. Everything has been seized and sold; and we have been changing about from lodging to lodging, for Cyril did not wish to be seen."

"Not wish to be seen?"

"No, uncle, dear. He said the failure of

the firm was so painful to him since Mr. Walker's death; and that the representatives of the poor old man had forced the estate into bankruptcy, and were behaving very badly to him."

"Humph!"

"People have behaved so very, very cruelly to him, and set about such dreadful stories; but you will not believe them, dear? He is my husband, and he has been very, very unfortunate."

"Very, my dear," said her uncle, drily.

"He has tried so hard," cried Sage, excitedly, "and fought so bravely to make a fortune; but the world has always been against him, do what he would."

"Hah, yes," said the Churchwarden, with a sigh. "But if people would be content with a good living, and not want to make fortunes, what trouble would be saved."

"Oh, don't: pray don't you turn against him, uncle, dear," sobbed Sage, piteously.

"No, my child," said the Churchwarden, gazing tenderly in her sad, thin face. "I shall not turn against him for your sake. But you had better tell me all. You say he is in trouble, but innocent?"

She gazed wildly from one to the other.

"I dare not," she moaned, as she covered her face with her hands, and shuddered.

"Dare not?"

"Yes, I dare," she cried, proudly throwing up her head. "It is not true. Cyril has his faults, but it is a cruel invention of spiteful enemies. It is a lie."

She stood up proudly defiant, ready to fight the world on her husband's behalf, and seemed half angry with her uncle's want of enthusiasm as he said, quietly—

"Tell me then, my dear. What do they say?"

"That he has committed forgery, and robbed poor old Mr. Walker, who, they say, died of a broken heart at the disgrace of the failure."

"And where is Cyril, now?" said the Churchwarden, whose forehead had grown full of deeper lines.

"Oh, uncle," Sage cried, throwing herself upon her knees, and shuddering as she covered her face with her hands. "He was sitting with me last night, and—Oh, I cannot bear it, I cannot bear it," she wailed—"the police came. They said it was a warrant, and—oh, uncle, help me, pray help me, for I have but you to cling to. My husband is in prison now. What shall I do?"

CHAPTER III.

LUKE ROSS HEARS NEWS.

OLD Michael Ross sat very patiently outside his son's chambers, watching the door, and finding enough satisfaction in reading over the name, ' Mr. Ross,' again and again.

" It's not a grand place to look at," he said to himself, " but they tell me he's growing quite a big man. I read for myself what he says to the judges in court sometimes ; and it's a very great thing for my son to be allowed to talk to them."

Then he had to move to allow some one to pass up, and soon after he had again to move for some one to pass down, and each time he rose those who passed looked keenly at the countrified old gentleman, with his carpet-bag and umbrella, but no one spoke.

" I did see how many people there are in London," said the old man to himself. " Three millions, I think it was; and yet what a strange dull place it is, and how lonesome a man can feel. Ah!" he said, sadly, "if my son was to be vexed because I have come up, and not be glad to see me, I think I should seem to be all alone in the world."

Just then the door opened, and the little clerk came out with a felt hat stuck very much on one side of his head.

He started as he saw the old man seated patiently waiting, and after closing the door he said, sharply—

"Now then, old chap, what are you stopping for?"

"I was waiting to see my—to see Mr. Ross," said the old man, who seemed quite humbled by the greatness of his son.

"Didn't I tell you he wasn't at home?" said the boy.

"Yes, sir; and I was going to wait till he returned."

"It's of no use to wait; he don't want to see you."

"Do you think not?" said the old man, humbly.

"I'm sure he don't.   What have you got to
sell?"

"Skins, sir, skins, principally sheep," said
the tanner, respectfully.

"Well, look here : just you be off.   The
governor buys all his skins when he wants 'em
at the law stationers, but he hardly ever uses
one.   It's the solicitors who do that.   Now
then, off you go."

Just then the door opened, and a well-
known voice called "Dick" loudly, the speaker
coming out on to the stone landing, and then
starting with surprise.

"Why, father!" he exclaimed.   "You here?
I am glad to see you.   Really, I *am* glad to
see you."

The grave, stern way of speaking was gone,
and it was Luke Ross of a dozen years before
who was shaking the old man by the hands,
and then patting him affectionately on the
shoulders, the old man dropping umbrella and
bag, and the tears starting to his weak old
eyes, as he saw his son's genuine pleasure at
the encounter.

"Come along in, father," continued Luke.

" Here, Dick, pick up those things and bring them in."

Dick screwed up his face and stared.

" I—I'll pick them up, Luke, my boy," quavered the old man, glancing at the young clerk.

" No, no; he'll bring them in, father," said Luke, drawing the old man into the office and into his private room, where he thrust him into the most comfortable chair, and then stood over him smiling with pleasure, seeming as if he could hardly make enough of the little, shrunken old man.

" Just come up, I suppose ?" cried Luke.

" Yes, my boy, yes," said old Michael, wiping his eyes; " but I've been sitting out there on the stairs these two hours."

" Sitting out there ! Why didn't you ring?"

" I did knock, my boy, and that lad of yours said you were out, and told me to go away; and if I had known you were in all the time, my boy, I should have gone away thinking you didn't want to see your old father. Did you tell him to say you were out, Luke ?"

" The young scoundrel ! no," cried Luke.

"I'm afraid he's a very wicked boy, then," piped the old man, "a very wicked boy. But are you glad to see me again, Luke?"

"Glad to see you, my dear old father? Why, yes, yes, you know I am. Come, come, come, or you'll make me weak too."

"Ye—ye—yes, my boy, it is weak," quavered the old fellow, wiping his eyes hastily; "but I'm getting very old now, Luke. 1 was a middle-aged man when I married your dear mother, and I'm seventy-nine now, and not so strong as I was, and—and I got fancying as I came up that now you had grown to be such a great man you wouldn't want to see such a shabby old fellow as I am at your chambers."

"For shame, father!" cried Luke, reproach-fully. "What cause have I ever given you for thinking that?"

"None at all, my boy, none at all. God bless you! You're a good lad, and I'm very proud of you, Luke, very proud of you, and —and I am so glad to see you again. Luke, my boy," he said, rising, and his tremulous old hands played caressingly about his son's shoulders, "I'm a very old fellow now, and I dare say this is the last time I shall come to town."

"Oh, no, no, no, father, you'll make plenty of journeys up yet."

"No, my boy, no," said the old fellow, calmly; and he shook his head. "It can't be; my next journey may be the long one, never to come back again, my boy."

"Oh, father, come, come," cried Luke, "don't talk like that."

"Why not, my boy?" said the old man, smiling; "it must come to that soon, and it never seems to trouble me now; but, Luke, my boy, would you—would you mind this once if—if I—if I—you were a little boy once, Luke, and I have always been so proud of you, and though you—you have grown to be such a great man, you seem only my boy still, and I should like to once more before I die."

"Like to what, father?" cried the young man, smiling at his elder's affectionate earnestness.

"I should like to kiss you, my boy—for the last time," faltered the old man, humbly.

"My dear old father!"

It was all that was heard save a muffled

sob, as Luke strained the old man to his breast, and position—the present—all was forgotten, as father and son stood there feeling as if five-and-twenty years had dropped away.

"Now," said Luke, as the old man, with a happy smile upon his face, resumed his chair, the younger half seating himself upon the writing-table before him. "Now then, father," said Luke, merrily, "am I glad to see you?"

"Yes, yes, my boy, I know you are;" and the old man took one of the delicate white hands in his, and gazed round the room. "I like your new chambers, my boy. Much better than the old ones. The furniture's very nice; but you never wrote to your poor old father for fifty or a hundred pounds to buy it," he said, reproachfully.

"There was no need, father," said Luke, smiling. "I am making a good deal of money now."

"Are you though? I'm glad of it. You ought to: you're so clever; but you never come down, my boy."

Luke's brow clouded.

"I haven't the heart, father," he said, after

a pause. "Come and see me instead; and if I don't write so often as I should, it is really because I spend so much time in study and hard work."

"Yes, of course, my boy, so you must. But—but you haven't asked me why I came up."

"To see me, of course," said Luke.

"Well, yes, my boy, I did; but you—you haven't the heart to come down?"

Luke shook his head.

"Do you—do you think,"—the old man held his son's hand in both his own, and looked timidly in his face, "do you think about her still, my boy?"

"Every day, father," said the young man, sternly. "I always shall."

"Yes, yes, my boy. That is why I came up. I came to tell you, my boy: she's in very great trouble."

"Trouble!" said Luke, quickly; and his voice sounded hoarse and strange—"again?"

"Yes, yes, my boy. I knew you would like to know."

Luke snatched his hand away, and paced

up and down the room several times before
stopping in front of the old man once more.

"Has—has she been down, father?"

"Yes, my boy, she came down with her
two little girls."

"Did you see her?" said Luke, hoarsely.

"Yes. my boy. I had to go to Churchwarden Portlock about some skins, and he
took me into the room where she was, and
she shook hands. Poor girl, poor girl, she's
strange and changed."

"Changed, father?"

"Yes; old and careworn. and as if she'd
suffered a deal of trouble."

Luke Ross's head went down upon his
breast, and his voice was almost inaudible as
he said—

"What is her trouble now?"

"You have heard nothing, then, my boy?"

"No, father, nothing."

"Not that the wine merchant's business has
all come to bankruptcy?"

"No, father; but I am not surprised. He
will always be a beggar. That is her trouble,
then. She is back home?"

"Oh, no, my boy; she is in London. She would not leave her husband. Churchwarden Portlock came up with her, for it is a terrible trouble this time."

"Indeed, father! Why?"

"They say he has committed forgery, my boy, and done no end of ill, and—and——"

"And what, father?" cried Luke, whose eyes were flashing with eagerness.

"He has been cast into prison, my boy, and they say it is a terribly bad case."

CHAPTER IV.

AN IMPORTANT BRIEF.

LUKE ROSS sat on the edge of his table for a few minutes gazing into vacancy, and at times it was with a look akin to triumph that he pondered upon the fall of the man who had been his one enemy—him who had seemed to turn the whole current of his life.

But as the old man watched his countenance, a sadder, softer mood came over it, and he said, as he turned once more to meet his father's eyes—

"Poor girl! It is terrible, indeed."

"Very, very terrible, my boy; and they say poor Mrs. Mallow is dying. Surely our poor parson has much to bear—much, indeed, to bear."

There was a few minutes' silence, and then

Luke turned to his father, and his lips moved to speak, but no words came for a time. At last he said—

"Do you know where Mrs. Cyril Mallow is staying, father?"

"Yes, my boy. Portlock told me, and asked me to go and see them if I came up."

"Go, then, father, and if you can help him, do so. I cannot go, but you—you could. Help Mr. Portlock if you can, and come to me for what you require. Poor girl," he added, to himself, "what a fate it is. Poor girl—poor girl!"

"I—I didn't think you would take on about it quite so much, my boy; but I thought I ought to tell you about it all."

"Yes, yes, father; it was quite right. I am glad you came up."

"It's—it's all about money, my boy, that Cyril Mallow has got into trouble."

"Yes, father, I suppose so," said Luke, whose thoughts were evidently in another direction.

"I liked Sage Portlock—I always did like her, my boy; and as you are getting on so well, and don't want the money I've scraped up for you, I wouldn't mind helping her in her trouble."

" It's very good of you, father," said the young man, smiling sadly.

" But it would be like pouring money into a well if her husband gets hold of it."

" If it is a case such as you describe, father," said Luke, thoughtfully, " I doubt whether money would be of much good."

The old man looked very anxiously at his son, even with a kind of awe, as if he were afraid of him.

" I don't like to ask him," he muttered, " I don't like to ask him ; " and he took out his old faded handkerchief and began nervously wiping his hands upon it, till Luke, in his abstraction, turned his eyes upon him with a vacant look that gradually became intense, as his father grew more nervous and troubled of mien.

As the old man shrank and avoided the gaze which drew him back, as it were, to look appealingly in the stern, searching eyes of his son, Luke spoke to him with the sharpness of one trying to master an evading witness, so that the old man started as the young barrister exclaimed—

"What is it, father? You are keeping something back."

"I—I hardly liked to say it, my boy. Don't be angry with me."

"Angry with you! What nonsense, father. But speak out. What is it? You want to say something to me."

"Ye—es, my boy, I do. But give me your hand, and don't speak so sharp and angrily to me. I'm—I'm getting old and nervous now. and a very little seems to upset me. I don't even like to walk amongst the tan-pits now, where I used to run without being a bit afraid. Thank you. my boy, thank you," he continued, nervously, as Luke caught and held his hand.

"It's a way I have of speaking, father," he said. "Angry? With you? Why my dear father, how could I be?"

"I—I don't know, my boy; but you promise me that you won't be angry?"

"Not a bit, father," cried Luke, with assumed cheeriness. "There, dad, I promise

you I won't even be cross if you have been
and married a young wife."

"Me? Married a young wife? Ha! ha!
ha! That's very funny of you, my boy, very
funny; but I haven't done that, Luke; I haven't
done that. I married at eight-and-thirty,
Luke, and once was enough. But you won't
be angry?"

"No, no, not a bit. Now come, confess.
What is it? I hope you haven't been invest-
ing in some shaky company."

"Oh no, my boy, not I. My bit of money
has all been put in land, every hundred I
could spare out of the business. But you said,
my boy, you—you wanted to help Mrs. Cyril."

Luke's countenance changed again, but he
nodded, and said hastily—

"Yes, father, of course. What can I do?"

"She—she said——"

"Who? Mrs. Cyril Mallow?"

"Yes, my boy," said the old man, clinging
to him. "Mrs. Cyril, she—she asked me to
come and see you."

"Sage — Mrs. Mallow did?" cried Luke,
sharply.

"You promised me, my boy, that you would not be cross with me," quavered the old man.

"No, no, father, I am not cross, but you startled me by your words. Did she tell you to come to me?"

"Yes, my boy, she—she's sadly altered, Luke, and so sweet and so humble. She wanted to go down on her knees to me, my boy, but I wouldn't let her."

"Tell me all, father," cried Luke. "Why are you keeping this back?"

"I—I daren't tell you, my boy, at first; I dare not, indeed."

"Tell me now, quickly."

"She told me to come to you, my boy; she said she had heard what a great counsel you had become."

Luke made an impatient movement.

"And she said that she had no one to appeal to in her sore distress."

"I am not her friend," said Luke, coldly.

"But you will be, my boy, when I tell you that, sobbing bitterly, she asked me to come to you, and if you had one spark of feeling for her left, to try and save her husband."

"She bade you come and say this, father?" cried Luke, with the beads of perspiration standing upon his brow.

"Yes, my son, for the sake of old times when you were girl and boy together."

Luke drew his hand away, and leaping from the edge of the table where he had been sitting, began to pace the room once more, while the old man sat rubbing his hands up and down his knees and gazing at him aghast.

Just then there was a sharp knock, and the boy entered.

"Engaged," said Luke, angrily. "I can see no one;" and the boy disappeared as if in alarm.

"I'm very, very sorry, my boy," faltered old Michael; "but ——"

Luke stopped before him in his hurried walk.

"Tell me again, father. Did Sage Mallow say those words?"

"Yes, my boy, almost word for word. She said she was in despair, that money could not help her, she wanted some one to save her husband."

"Not to help her," said Luke, bitterly, "but to save that man."

"Yes, my boy. It's very shocking, for I'm afraid he's a dreadful scamp; but you know what women are."

"Yes," said Luke, with a laugh that startled his father, "I know what women are."

"The bigger scamp a man is the more they hold by him. Perhaps it's quite right, but it's very shocking."

"Help her to save him," muttered Luke. "I can't do it. I can—not do it."

The old man had now rolled his handkerchief up into a ball, and was pressing it and kneading it between his hands, as he gazed helplessly in his son's face.

"I think if she had seen you, and asked you herself, you would have done it, Luke, my boy. She said that she believed you could save her husband, and that if he was condemned——"

"I tell you if he were ten times condemned," cried Luke, "I could not do it, father. It is madness to ask me, of all men, to fight on his behalf."

"He—he did behave very badly to you, my boy. He's a bad one, I'm afraid; but he is that poor creature's husband."

"The only enemy I ever had, and you ask me to save him. It is not in human nature to do it. Why do you come and ask me such a thing?"

"You said you would not be angry with me, Luke; and she begged of me so hard, for the sake of the very old times, she said; and then she broke down, and said that if anything happened to her husband she should die."

Luke walked to the window, and stood gazing out at the narrow lane below, with a great struggle going on in his breast. In his heart there was still left so tender an affection for Sage that he was ready to save her. For her sake he had given no thought to another of her sex, eschewing society, and devoting himself constantly to his profession; and now that his father had raised up before him, as it were, the face of the suffering wife, piteous and appealing, as she sent to him her message, asking, for the sake of old days, that he would come to her help, he felt that he must go—must devote his powers to saving the man she loved.

But it was impossible. He could not. He would not. He was but a man, he told himself, and this would be the work of an angel. No; he hated Cyril Mallow intensely, as the man who had robbed him of all he held dear, at the same time that he despised him in his honourable heart as a contemptible scoundrel who would sacrifice any one to gain his own ends.

Luke was not surprised to hear of Cyril being in fresh difficulties; he was ready, also, to believe that he was guilty, and he was asked to become this man's advocate, to bring to bear his twelve years' hard study and self-denial to try and save him from some richly-merited punishment. It was too much.

As he stood there, gazing out of the window, he seemed to see Cyril's mocking, handsome, triumphant face, as he made him also his slave —one of those whose duty it was to try and drag him from the slough as soon as ever he thought proper to step in—one of those who were to lie down, that he might plant his foot upon the bended neck, step out into safety, and leave the helper in the mire.

On the other hand, strive to exclude it as he would, there was Sage's appealing face, not the sweet girlish countenance he knew, but a face chastened by suffering, full of trust in him as in one who could and would help her in this supreme time of her trouble.

He fought against it, but in vain. He told himself that he should be mad to take up such a cause; that men would sneer and say evil things of him—that it was from no disinterested motives that he had done this thing; but there was ever the appealing face, the soft pleading eyes seeming to say to him, "I was weak and foolish, as well as cruel, in choosing as I did, but I humble myself now into the very dust, and ask you to forgive me and come to my help."

Her very words seemed to say as much, and a strange thrill of triumph ran through him, as his eyes flashed, and for the moment he gloried in Cyril Mallow's disgrace.

He put away the thoughts, though, as a shame unto him, and folding his arms, he tried to master himself, to get his mental balance once again, for it was terribly disturbed by the strange access of emotion that he felt.

No, he said, when he went down to Kilby Farm on that never-to-be-forgotten day, Sage Portlock's life and his own, that had run on together for so long, had suddenly diverged, and they had been growing farther and farther apart ever since. He could not do this thing. It was impossible. It was a fresh act of cruelty on Sage's part, and come what might he would not degrade himself by fighting Cyril Mallow's cause, only afterwards, if he saved him, to reap the scoundrel's contempt.

"And I should deserve it," he said, half aloud.

"Yes, my boy," quavered old Michael, eagerly, as he caught his son's words and interpreted them to his own wishes. "God bless you, my boy, I knew you would. and she said she knew your good and generous heart. and that night by night she would teach her little ones to love and reverence your name, as they knelt down and prayed for God's blessing on him who saved their father from disgrace."

Luke Ross had opened his lips to stop his father's enthusiastic words, when his excited fancy pictured before him the soft, sweet, care-worn face of Sage, his old love, bending over her innocent children, and teaching them, as she held their little clasped hands, to join his name in their trusting prayers, and he was conquered.

He dared not turn, for his face was convulsed, but, sinking sidewise into a chair, he rested his head upon his arm, and, hearing his father approach, motioned with the hand that was free, for him to keep back.

But the old man did not heed the sign. He came forward and laid his trembling hand upon his son's head.

"God bless you, my noble boy!" he said, fervently. "I knew you would."

Neither spoke then for a time, and when Luke raised his face once more, it was very pale, as if he were exhausted by the fight.

"Why, father," he said, cheerfully, "I'm

behaving very badly to you. You must want something to eat."

"No, my boy, I had something before I came in, for fear I should put you out. I don't want anything else."

"'Till dinner-time, father," said Luke, smiling. "You and I will dine together and enjoy ourselves."

"But that poor woman, Luke?"

"We'll settle all that, father, after dinner. You shall give me the address, and I will either get a fresh solicitor to take the matter up or consult with theirs."

"But won't you fight for them, my boy?"

"To be sure I will, father, and do my best. But you don't understand these matters; an attorney has to draw up the brief."

"Of course, yes, of course, my boy."

"He brings it to me like this," said Luke, taking up the one he had been studying, "with all the principal points of the case neatly written out, as a sort of history, giving me the particulars necessary, so that I can master them in a quick, concise way."

"Yes, I see, my boy."

"A good lawyer will, in consultation with his client, clear away all superfluous matter, leaving nothing but what is necessary for the counsel to know."

"Yes, my son, same as we first of all get rid of the refuse from a skin."

"Exactly, father," said Luke, smiling; "for clients often think matters of great moment that are worthless in a court of law."

"To be sure, yes; people will talk too much, my boy, I know," said the old man. "Why, Lukey, how I should like to hear you laying down the law in your wig and gown, my boy. How you must give it to 'em. I've read about you in the newspaper. Old Mr. Mallow always brings one to me when he sees your name in, and shakes hands with me; and the tears come in the old fellow's eyes as he says to me with a sigh, 'Ah, Mr. Ross, I wish I had had such a son.'"

"Why, father," said Luke, smiling, and seeming himself once more, "it is a good job that you don't live near me."

"Don't say that, my boy," said the old man,

looking quite aghast. "I—I was thinking how nice it would be if I could get nearer to you."

"You'd spoil me with flattery," said Luke.

"Nay, nay, my boy," said the old man, seriously. "I never told you aught but the truth, and if I saw a fault I'd out with it directly."

"You always were the best of fathers," cried Luke, clasping the old man's hand.

"And—and I thank God, my boy, for His blessings on my old age," quavered the old man, with the weak tears in his eyes—"You were always the best of sons."

They sat hand clasped in hand for a few moments, and then the old man said softly—

"God will bless you for your goodness to that poor woman, my boy. I know it has been a hard fight, but you have won. It is heaping coals of fire on your enemy's head to do good to him, and maybe afterwards Cyril Mallow may repent. But, Luke, my boy," he cried, cheerfully, "I'm a stupid old man, only you must humour me."

"How, father?"

" Let me see you, just for a minute, in your wig and gown."

" Nonsense, father !"

" But I should like it, my boy."

Luke rose to humour him, putting on wig and gown, and making the old man rub his hands with gratification as he gazed at the clear, intelligent face, with its deeply-set, searching eyes.

" I'll be bound to say you puzzle and frighten some of them, my boy," said the old man. " And that's a brief, is it ? "

" Yes, father," said Luke, smiling down on the old man, so full of childlike joy.

" Ah, yes," said the old man, putting on a pair of broad-rimmed spectacles, and then reading—" Jones v. Lancaster." " Hah ! yes, nicely written ; better than this fifty gs. What does that mean ? "

" Fifty guineas, father."

" Indeed ! And which was it, Jones or Lancaster, who stole the fifty guineas ? "

" Neither, father. That is a common-pleas case of some importance, and the fifty guineas is my fee."

"Your fee?" cried the old man. "You don't mean to tell me that you get fifty-two pounds ten shillings, my boy, for your fee?"

"Yes, father, I do now," said his son, smiling.

"Bless my soul! Why, Luke, you ought to grow rich."

"Well, I suppose so, father; but I don't much care. I should like to grow famous, and make myself a name."

"And you will, my boy—you will," cried the old man, as Luke slipped off his legal uniform, and replaced the wig and gown.

"Time proves all things, father."

"And may I look? I won't tell. Is this another brief?"

"Yes, father; I get plenty now."

"But—but—you are not paid fifty guineas a-piece for them, my boy?"

"Yes, father, I take nothing below that fee now, and even then I get more than I can undertake."

The old man threw himself back in his chair, and, after a struggle, drew out of his trousers pocket a reddish canvas bag, and untied the string around the neck.

"Why, what are you going to do, father?" said Luke.

"I'm going to pay my son the fee for the brief in Cyril Mallow's case, and I'm as proud as proud to have it to do."

"No, no," cried Luke; "that must not be."

"But I will, my boy, I will," said the old man.

"No, no, father, I could not take it. You would hurt me if you pressed it."

"But I've plenty of money, my boy."

"So have I, father, and I could not do my duty in that defence if it was a matter of payment. If I take that brief," he said, solemnly, "my payment is Sage Mallow's thanks and her children's prayers."

The old man sat thinking for a few moments.

"You are right, my boy, you are right," he said, replacing his bag. "And, of course, all I have is yours. But you will take the brief, Luke, my boy?"

"Yes, father, if I can I will."

"Then you will," cried the old man, joyously.

"Hah, let's look at that. It's a big one,
Luke;" and he picked up, with his eyes
sparkling with paternal pride, the brief brought
in that morning by Mr. Swift. "Hah! this
has been altered," said the old man. "It was
twenty-five guineas, and that's crossed out,
and they've written fifty. I'll bet twopence
they offered you twenty-five first, and you
wouldn't take it."

"Quite right, father," said Luke, upon
whom his father's enjoyment came like so
much sunshine in a dull life.

"Quite right, my boy, quite right. Let
'em know your value. You're a man of
business, Luke. Now, what's this, my
boy?"

"I really don't know, father, only that it is
for the prosecution in an important criminal
case."

"Criminal case, eh? And you haven't
studied it, then?"

"Not yet. I was going to finish Jones
versus Lancaster first."

"And this is *re* Esdaile, eh? What's that?
Esdaile, Esdaile, and Co. Why, that's the

name of the wine-merchants' firm where Cyril Mallow was partner."

"*What?*" roared Luke.

He snatched the brief from his father's hand, tore it open, and as the leaves fluttered in his trembling hand he sank back in a chair, looking like one who had received some deadly blow.

CHAPTER V.

A HARD DUTY.

OLD Michael Ross was at his son's side on the instant.

"Are you ill, my boy? Tell me what it is! You frighten me, Luke!—you frighten me!"

"I shall be better directly, father," panted Luke, with a strange look in his face.

"But you are ill. Let me send for brandy."

"No, no; I am better now! It is nothing. But tell me, father, I thought that man became partner with a Mr. Walker?"

"Yes, my boy; I believe it was a very old firm, trading as Esdaile and Co. No other names appeared."

"Good heavens!" muttered Luke, who kept glancing at the brief and turning over its leaves.

"Why, Luke!" exclaimed the old man, excitedly, as the state of the case flashed upon him. "You are not already engaged in this affair?"

"I am, father," he said, with a strange pallor gathering in his face. "I have undertaken the prosecution of Cyril Mallow on behalf, it seems, of Mr. Walker's executors, and I shall have to try and get him convicted."

Father and son sat gazing blankly in each other's eyes, thinking of the future; and as Luke pondered on the position into which he had been thrown by fate, he saw that he should be, as it were, the hand of Nemesis standing ready to strike the heartless spendthrift down—that he was to be his own avenger of the wrongs that he had suffered from his enemy, and that no greater triumph could be his than that of pointing out, step by step, to the jury, the wrongdoings of this man, who would be standing in the felon's dock quailing before him, looking in his eyes for mercy, but finding none.

He shuddered at the picture, for soon fresh faces appeared there—that of Sage, standing

with supplicating hands and with her tearful,
dilated eyes, seeming to ask him for pity for
her children's sake. Then he saw the white-
haired rector gazing at him piteously, and the
suffering invalided mother who worshipped
her son. Both were there, asking him what
they had done that he should seek to convict
him they loved.

He looked up, and saw that his father was
watching him with troubled face.

"This—this is very terrible, my boy," he
said. "I ought to have been sooner. But—
but—must you take that side?"

"I have promised, father. I would give
anything to have been under the same promise
to you. But I cannot, I will not stand up
and accuse Cyril Mallow. Strive how I
would, I should fight my hardest to get a
verdict against him, and I could not afterwards bear the thought. I will get off taking
this brief. Stay here while I go out."

He took his hat, and was driven to his
solicitors, where he had an interview with
Mr. Swift, and proposed that that gentleman
should retire the brief from his hands.

Mr. Swift smiled, and shook his head.

"No, Mr. Ross," he said; "I have given you your price, and after a chat with my partner, he agreed that I had done right. The matter is settled, sir! I could not hear of such a thing."

Luke was in no mood to argue with him then, but went back to his chambers, dined with his father, and then sat up half the night studying the brief, not with the idea of being for the prosecution, but so as to know how Cyril Mallow stood.

It was a long brief, and terrible in its array of charges against Sage's husband. As he read on, Luke found that the executors of Cyril's partner, the late Mr. Walker, were determined upon punishing him who had wrought his ruin. The wine business had been a good and very lucrative one until Mr. Walker had been tempted into taking a partner, whose capital had not been needed, the object really being to find a junior who would relieve the senior from the greater part of the anxiety and work.

Cyril then had been received into the

partnership, and a great deal of the management had after a short time been left to him, a position of which he took advantage to gamble upon the Stock Exchange with the large sums of money passing through their hands, with just such success as might have been expected, and the discovery that Cyril had involved the firm in bankruptcy broke Mr. Walker's heart, the old man dying within a week of the schedule being filed.

Worse was behind: the executors charged Cyril with having forged his partner's name to bills, whereon he had raised money, signing not merely the name of the firm, but his own and his partner's name, upon the strength of which money had been advanced by two bill discounters, both of whom were eager to have him punished.

In short, the more Luke Ross studied, the more he found that the black roll of iniquity was unfolding itself, so that at last he threw down the brief, heartsick with disgust and misery, feeling as he did that if half, nay, a tithe of that which was charged against Cyril were true, no matter who conducted prosecution or defence, the jury was certain to convict him of downright forgery and swindling, and seven or ten years' penal servitude would be his sentence.

It needed no dull, cheerless morning for Luke's spirits to be at the lowest ebb when he met his father at breakfast, the old man looking very weak, careworn, and troubled, as they sat over the barely-tasted meal.

Luke hardly spoke, but sat there thinking that he would make a fresh appeal to Mr. Swift to relieve him of so terrible a charge, and expecting each moment that his father would again implore him to retire from the prosecution and take up the defence. At last the old man spoke.

"I've been lying awake all night, thinking about that, my boy," he said, "and I'm very, very sorry."

"Father," said Luke, "it seems almost more than one can bear."

"I said to myself that my boy was too noble not to forgive one who had done wrong to him in the past, and I said, too, that it would be a fine thing for him to show people how he was ready to go and fight on his old rival's behalf."

"And I will, father, or retire from the case altogether," said Luke, eagerly.

"No, my son, no," said the old man; "I have not long to live, and I should not like that little time to be embittered by the thought that I had urged my son to do a dishonourable act."

"Oh, no," cried Luke, "I will press them, and they will let me retire."

"But if they refused again, my boy, it would be dishonourable to draw back after you had promised to do your best. No, my boy, there is the finger of God in it all, and you must go on. Poor girl, poor girl! it will be terrible for her, but we cannot fight against such things."

"But I could not plead my cause with her eyes reproaching me," said Luke, half to himself.

"But you must, my boy," cried the old man. "I lay awake all last night, Luke, and I prayed humbly for guidance to do what was right, and it seemed to me that the good counsel came."

"Father!" exclaimed Luke, gazing in the old man's face.

"It will be painful, my boy, but we must not shrink from our duty because it is a difficult one to perform. I am a weak old fellow, and very ignorant, but I know that here my son will be a minister of justice against a bad and wicked man. For he is a bad—a wicked man, my boy, who has stopped at nothing to gratify his own evil ends."

"But how can I proceed against him, father?"

"Because it is your duty; and, feeling what you do against him, you will guard your heart lest you should strike too hard; and it is better so. Luke, my boy, you will be just; while, if another man prosecutes him, he will see in him only the forger and the cheat, and fight his best to get him condemned."

It was true, and Luke sat back thinking.

"Yesterday, my boy, I prayed you to undertake this man's defence; I withdraw it all now: take back every word, and I will go and tell poor Sage Mallow why."

"No, no, father," cried Luke; "if I cannot defend, neither will I prosecute."

"You must, my boy—you have given your word. If you drew back now I should feel that it would go worse against this man."

"But mine, father, should not be the hand to strike him down," cried Luke.

"We are not our own masters here, my boy," said the old man, speaking in a low and reverent tone. "My Luke has never shrunk from his duty yet, and never will."

Luke sank back in silence, and for a long time no word was spoken. Then he suddenly rose and rang the bell.

"See if Mr. Serjeant Towle is in," he said to the boy, and upon the report being received that the serjeant was within, Luke descended and had ten minutes' conversation with that great legal luminary, who, after a little consideration, said, as Luke rose to go—

"Well, yes, Ross, I will, if it's only for the sake of giving you a good thrashing. You are going on too fast, and a little check will do you good. If I take the brief I shall get him off. Send his solicitors to me."

Five minutes later Luke was with his father.

"Go and see Mrs. Mallow at once, father," he said, "and bid her tell her solicitors to wait upon Mr. Serjeant Towle."

"Yes, my boy—Mr. Serjeant Towle," said the old man, obediently.

"He will require an enormous fee, father, which you will pay."

"Yes, my boy, of course. Is—is he a great man?"

"One of the leading counsel at the bar; and if Cyril Mallow can be got off, Serjeant Towle is the man for the task."

"But, my boy——" began the old man.

"Don't hesitate, father, but go," cried Luke; and the old man hurried off.

CHAPTER VI.

THE CASE FOR THE PROSECUTION.

It was a strange stroke of fate that, in spite of several attempts to evade the duty. circumstances so arranged themselves that Luke Ross found himself literally forced, for his reputation's sake, to go on with his obnoxious task, and at last the day of trial came.

Luke had passed a sleepless night, and he entered the court, feeling excited, and as if all before him was a kind of dream.

For a few minutes he had not sufficient self-possession even to look round the well of the building; and it was some time before he ventured to scan the part that would be occupied by the spectators. Here, however, for the time being, his eyes remained riveted.

as a choking sensation attacked him, for, seated beside the sturdy, well-remembered figure of the Churchwarden, was a careworn, youngish woman, so sadly altered that Luke hardly recognized her as the Sage whose features were so firmly printed on his memory.

She evidently did not see him, but was watching the jury-box, and listening to some remarks made to her from time to time by her uncle.

Luke turned over his brief, and tried to think of what he could do to be perfectly just, and yet spare the husband of the suffering woman before him, and at whom he gazed furtively from time to time.

He saw her as through a mist, gazing wildly at the judge, and then at the portly form and florid face of Serjeant Towle, who was now engaged in an eager conversation with his junior; and the sight of the famous legal luminary for the moment cleared away the misty dreaminess of the scene. Luke's pulses began to throb, and he felt like one about to enter the arena for a struggle. He had had many legal battles before, from out of which, through his quickness in seizing upon damaging points, he had come with flying colours; but he had never before been opposed to so powerful an adversary as the serjeant, and, for the moment, a strong desire to commence the encounter came over him.

But this passed off, and the dreamy sensation came back, as he sat gazing at Sage, thinking of their old childish days together, their .walks in the wold woodlands, flower-gathering, nutting, or staining their hands with blackberries; of the many times when he climbed the orchard trees to throw down the ripening pears to Sage, who spread her pinafore to receive them. In these dreamy thoughts the very sunshine and sleepy atmosphere of the old place came back, and the sensation of remembrance of the old and happy days became a painful emotion.

It must be a dream, he felt. That could not be Sage seated there by the sturdy, portly, grey-haired man, her uncle. Even old Michael Ross seemed to be terribly changed, making it impossible that the little, thin, withered man seated behind Churchwarden Portlock could be the quick, brisk tradesman of the past.

"Was it all true?" Luke kept asking himself, "or was it, after all, but a dream?"

Cyril Mallow's was the first case to be taken that morning, and the preliminaries were soon settled; but all the while the dreaminess of the scene seemed to Luke to be on the increase. He tried to bring his thoughts back from the past, but it was impossible; and when Mr. Swift the solicitor who had instructed him spoke, the words seemed to be a confused murmur from far away.

Then the clerk of arraigns called the prisoner's name, and as Cyril Mallow was placed at the bar, and Luke gazed at the face that had grown coarse and common-looking in the past twelve years, the dreaminess increased still more.

Luke was conscious of rising to bow to the court and say, "I am for the prosecution, my lord"; and heard the deep, rolling, sonorous voice of Mr. Serjeant Towle reply, "I am for the defence, my lord"; and then Luke's eyes rested upon Sage, who for the first time recognized him, and was now leaning forward, looking at him with wild and starting eyes that seemed to implore him to spare her husband, for the sake of their childhood's days; and her look fascinated him so that he could not tear his gaze away.

It must be a dream, or else he was ill, for there was now a strange singing in his ears, as well as the misty appearance before his eyes, through which he could see nothing but Sage Portlock, as his heart persisted in calling her still.

"Was he to go on?" he asked himself, "to go wading on through this terrible nightmare, planting sting after sting in that tender breast, or should he give it up at once?"

He wanted to—he strove to speak, and say, "My lord, I give up this prosecution," but his lips would not utter the words. For he was in a nightmare-like dream, and no longer a free agent.

And yet his nerves were so overstrung that he was acutely conscious of the slightest sound in the court, as he rose now, the observed of all present.

He heard the soft, subdued rustle made by people settling in their places for the long trial; the catching, hysterical sigh uttered by the prisoner's wife; and a quick, faint cough, or clearing of the throat, as the prisoner leaned against the dock, and sought to get rid of an unpleasant, nervous contraction of the throat.

Luke stood like one turned to stone, his eyes now fixed on vacancy, his brief grasped in his hand, and his face deadly pale. The moment had arrived for him to commence the prosecution, but his thoughts were back at Lawford, and, like a rapid panorama, there passed before his eyes the old schoolhouses, and the figure of the bright, clever young mistress in the midst of her pupils, while he seemed to hear their merry voices as they darted out into the sunshine, dismissed for the day.

Then he was studying for the mastership, and was back at the training college. That was not the judge seated on his left, but the vice-principal, and those were not spectators and reporters ranged there, tier above tier, with open books and ready pencils, but fellow-students; and he was down before them, at the great black board, helpless and ashamed, for the judge—no, it was the vice-principal—had called him down from his seat, and said—

"If any right-angled triangle the square of the sides subtending the right angle is equal to the square of the sides containing the right angle.   Prove it."

Prove it!   And that forty-seventh problem of the first book of Euclid that he knew so well had gone, as it were, right out of his memory, leaving but a blank.

There was a faint buzz and rustle amongst the students as it seemed to him in this waking nightmare, and the vice-principal said—

"We are all ready, Mr. Ross."

Still not a word would come.   Some of the students would be, he knew, pitying him, not knowing how soon their own turn might come, while others he felt would be triumphant, being jealous of his bygone success.

He knew that book so well, too; and somehow Sage Portlock had obtained a seat amongst the students, and was waiting to hear him demonstrate the problem, drawing it with a piece of chalk on the black board, and showing how the angle A B C was equal to the angle D E F, and so on, and so on.

"We are all ready, Mr. Ross," came from the vice-principal again. No, it was from the judge, and it was not the theatre at St. Chrysostom's, but the court at the Old Bailey, where he was to prosecute Cyril Mallow, his old rival, the husband of the woman he had loved, for forgery and fraud; and his throat was dry, his tongue clave to the roof of his mouth, and his thoughts were wandering away.

And yet his senses were painfully acute to all that passed. He knew that Serjeant Towle had chuckled fatly, after fixing his great double eyeglass to gaze at him. Then, as distinctly as if the words were uttered in his ear, he heard one of the briefless whisper—

"He has lost his nerve."

There was an increase in the buzzing noise, and an usher called out loudly, "Silence."

"Ross, Mr. Ross! For heaven's sake go on," whispered Mr. Swift, excitedly; and Luke felt a twitching at his gown.

But he could not master himself. It was

still all like a nightmare, when he turned his eyes slowly on the judge, but in a rapt, vacant way, for the old gentleman said kindly—

"I am afraid you are unwell, Mr. Ross."

Luke was conscious of bowing slightly, and just then a hysterical sigh from the over-wrought breast of Sage struck upon his ear, and he was awake once more.

The incident had been most painful, and to a man the legal gentlemen had considered it a complete breakdown of one of the most promising of the young legal stars, those who had been so far disappointed seeing in the downfall of a rival a chance for themselves.

But the next minute all that had passed was looked upon as a slight eccentricity on the part of a rising man. Mr. Swift, who had begun to grind his teeth with annoyance, thrust both his hands into his great blue bag, as if in search of papers, but so as to be able to conceal the gratified rub he was giving them, as he heard Luke Ross in a clear incisive tone, and with a gravity of mien and bearing beyond his years, state the case for the prose-cution in a speech that lasted quite a couple of hours. Too long, some said, but it was so masterly in its perspicuity, and dealt so thoroughly with the whole case, that it was finally declared to be the very perfection of forensic eloquence.

How his lips gave utterance to the speech Luke himself hardly knew, but with his father's words upon his duty ringing in his ears, he carried out that duty as if he had neither feeling against the prisoner, nor desire to save him from his well-merited fate. With the strict impartiality of one holding the scales of justice poised in a hand that never varied in its firmness for an instant, he laid bare Cyril Mallow's career as partner in the wine firm, and showed forth as black an instance of ingratitude, fraud, and swindling as one man could have gathered into so short a space.

There was a murmur of applause as Luke took his seat. Then his junior called the first witness, and the trial dragged its slow length along; while Luke sat, feeling that Sage would never forgive him for the words that he had said.

Witness after witness, examination and

cross-examination, till the prosecution gave way to the defence, and Serjeant Towle shuffled his gown over his shoulders, got his wig awry, and fought the desperate cause with all his might.

But all in vain. The judge summed up dead against the prisoner, alluding forcibly to the kindly consideration of the prosecution; and after stigmatizing the career of Cyril Mallow as one of the basest, blackest ingratitude, and a new example of the degradation to which gambling would lead an educated man, he left the case in the jury's hands, these gentlemen retiring for a few minutes, and then returning with a verdict of guilty.

Sentence, fourteen years' penal servitude. And, once more, as in a dream, Luke saw Cyril Mallow's blotched face gazing at him full of malice, and a look of deadly hatred in his eyes, before he was hurried away.

He was then conscious of Mr. Swift saying something to him full of praise, and of Serjeant Towle leaning forward to shake hands, as he whispered—

"You beat me, Ross, thoroughly.   We'll be on the same side next time."

But the dreaminess was once more closing in Luke Ross as with a mist, and in it he saw a pale, agonized face gazing reproachfully in his direction as its owner was being helped out of the court.

" God help me ! " muttered Luke. " I must have been mad. She will think it was revenge, when I would sooner have died than given her pain."

CHAPTER VII.

AFTER THE SENTENCE.

THERE was nothing farther to detain Luke Ross, but he remained in his seat for some time, studying the next case people said, but only that he might dream on in peace, for in the midst of the business of the next trial he found repose. No one spoke to him, and he seemed by degrees to be able to condense his thoughts upon the past.

And there he sat, trying to examine himself searchingly, probing his every thought as he sought for condemnatory matter against himself.

He felt as if he had been acting all day under some strange influence, moved by a power that was not his own, and that, as the instrument in other hands, he had been employed to punish Cyril Mallow.

"They will all join in condemning me," he thought, "and henceforth I shall go through life branded as one who hounded down his enemy almost to the death."

At length he raised his eyes, and they rested upon the little, thin, wistful countenance of his father, and there was a feeling of bitter reproach for his neglect of one who had travelled all the previous day so as to be present at the trial.

He made a sign to him as he rose, and the old man joined him in the robing-room, where Mr. Dick eyed him askance as he relieved his master of his wig and gown; and then they returned to the chambers, where Luke threw himself into a chair, and gazed helplessly at his father, till the old man laid a hand, almost apologetically, upon his son's arm.

"You are tired out, my boy. Come with me, and let us go somewhere and dine."

"After I have disgraced myself like this, father?" groaned Luke. "Are you not ashamed of such a son?"

"Ashamed? Disgraced? My boy, what do you mean? I never felt so proud of you before. It was grand!"

"Proud!" cried Luke, passionately, "when I seem to have stooped to the lowest form of cowardly retaliation. A rival who made himself my enemy is grovelling in the mire, and I, instead of going to him like an honourable, magnanimous man, to raise him up and let him begin a better life, have planted my heel upon his face, and crushed him lower into the slough."

"It was your duty, my boy, and you did that duty," cried the old man, quickly. "I will not hear you speak like that."

"And Sage—his wife," groaned Luke, not hearing, apparently, his father's words. "Father, the memory of my old love for her has clung to me ever. I have been true to that memory, loving still the sweet, bright girl I knew before that man came between us like a black shadow and clouded the sunshine of my life."

He stopped, and let his head rest upon his hand.

"My love for her has never failed, father, but is as fresh and bright now as it was upon the day when I came up here to town ready for the long struggle I felt that I should have before I could seek her for my wife. That love, I tell you, is as fresh and warm now as it was that day, but it has always been the love of one suddenly cut off from me —the love of one I looked upon as dead. For that evening, when I met them in the Kilby lane, Sage Portlock died to me, and the days I mourned were as for one who had passed away."

"My boy, my boy, I know. He did come between you, and seemed to blight your life, but he is punished now."

"Punished? No," said Luke, excitedly; "it is not the man I have punished, but his wife. Father, that sorrowing, reproachful look she directed at me this morning will cling to me to my dying day. I cannot bear it. I feel as if the memory would drive me mad."

He started up, and paced the room in an agony of mind that alarmed old Michael, who sought in vain to utter soothing words.

At last, as if recalled to himself by the feeling that he was neglecting the trembling old man before him, Luke made an effort to master the thoughts that troubled him, and they were about to go out together, when the boy announced two visitors, and Luke shrank back unnerved once more, on finding that they were the Reverend Eli Mallow and his old Churchwarden.

"I did not know his father was in town," said Luke, in a low voice.

"Yes, my boy, he sat back, poor fellow. He looks very old and weak," said Michael Ross, in a quiet patronizing way. "He is a good deal broken, my boy. Speak kindly to him, pray."

"What do they want?" said Luke. "Oh, father, what have I done that fate should serve me such an ugly turn?"

"Your duty, my boy, your duty," whispered the old man; and the next minute the visitors were in the room, finding, as they entered, that old Michael was holding his son's arm in a tender, proud way that seemed to fix the old Rector's eyes.

He was, indeed, old-looking and broken; sadly changed from the fine, handsome, grey-headed man that Luke knew so well.

"I met Mr. Mallow almost at your door," said Portlock, in his bluff, firm way. "We did not come together, but we both wanted to call."

Luke pointed to chairs, but the old Rector remained standing, gazing reproachfully at Luke.

"Yes, I wanted to see you," he said; "I wanted to see and speak to the man I taught when he was a boy, and in whom I took a great deal of pride. I was proud to see you progress, Luke Ross. I used to read and show the reports to your father when I saw them, for I said Luke Ross is a credit to our town."

"And you said so to me often, Mr. Mallow," cried old Michael.

"I did—I did," said the Rector; "and to-day in court I asked myself what I had ever done to this man that he should strike me such a blow."

"Be just, for heaven's sake, Mr. Mallow,"

cried Luke. "I did not seek the task I have fulfilled to-day."

"And I said to myself, as I saw my only son dragged away by his gaolers, 'I will go and curse this man—this cold-blooded wretch who could thus triumph over us.' I said I would show him what he has done—bruised my heart, driven a suffering woman nearly mad, and made two little innocent children worse than orphans."

"Mr. Mallow, is this justice?" groaned Luke.

"No," said the old man, softly. "I said it in mine haste, and as I hurried here mine anger passed away; the scales dropped from mine eyes, and I knew that it was no work of thine. Truly, as Eli's sons of old brought heaviness to their father's heart, so have my poor sons to mine; and, Michael Ross," he cried, holding out his trembling hands, "I was so proud of that boy—so proud. He was his mother's idol, and, bad as he would be at times, he was always good to her. Can you wonder that she loved him? Oh, God help me! my boy—my boy!"

"It has been an agony to me ever since the brief was forced upon me, Mr. Mallow," said Luke, taking the old man's hand. "Believe me, I could not help this duty I had to do."

"God bless you, Luke Ross!" said the old man, feebly. "Like Balaam of old, I came to curse, and I stop to bless. If I have anything to forgive, I forgive you, as I hope to be forgiven. You have been a good son. Michael Ross, you have never known what it is to feel as I do now. But I must go back; I must go back to her at home. She waits to know the worst, and this last blow will kill her, gentlemen—my poor, suffering angel of a wife—it will be her death."

"Will you not come and see Sage first?" said Portlock, with rough sympathy.

"No, no, I think not. The sight of my sad face would do her harm. I'll get home. Keep her with you, Portlock. God bless her!—a true, sweet wife. We came like a blight to her, Portlock. Luke Ross, I ought not to have allowed it, but I thought it was for the best—that it would reform my boy. My life has been all mistakes, and I long now to lie down and sleep. Keep her with you, Portlock, and teach her and her little ones to forget us all."

He tottered to the door to go, but Luke stepped forward.

"He is not fit to go alone," he cried. "Mr. Portlock, what is to be done?"

"I must take him home," he replied, sadly. "I'd better take them all home, but I have a message for you."

"For me?" cried Luke. "Not from Mrs. Cyril?"

"Yes, from Sage. She wants to see you."

"I could not bear it," cried Luke. "Heavens, man! have I not been reproached enough?"

"It is not to reproach you, I think, Luke Ross," said Portlock, softly. "She bade me say to thee, 'Come to me, if you have any sympathy for my piteous case.'"

CHAPTER VIII.

A FORLORN HOPE.

"Come to me if you have any sympathy for my piteous case!"

Sympathy! In his bitter state of self-reproach, he would have done anything to serve her. He felt that he could forgive Cyril Mallow, aid him in any way, even to compromising himself by helping him to escape. But he shrank from meeting Sage: he felt that he could not meet her reproachful eyes.

"You will come and see her?" said the Churchwarden. "Ah, my lad, if we could have looked into the future!"

His voice shook a little as he spoke, but he seemed to nerve himself, and said again—

"You will come and see her?"

"If it will be any good. Yes," said Luke, slowly; and they proceeded together to the hotel, where Sage was staying with her uncle, in one of the streets leading out of the Strand.

The old Rector was so broken of spirit that he allowed Portlock to lead him like a child, and, satisfied with the assurance that to-morrow he should return home, he sat down in the room set apart, with old Michael Ross, while, in obedience to a sign from Portlock, Luke followed him to a room a few doors away.

The place was almost in shadow, for the gas had not been lit, and as Luke entered, with his heart beating fast, a dark figure rose from an easy-chair by the fire, and tottered towards the old farmer, evidently not seeing Luke, who stayed back just within the door.

"He would not come," she cried. "It was cruel of him. I thought he had a nobler heart, and in all these years would have forgiven me at last."

"Mr. Ross is here, Sage," said Portlock, rather sternly. "Shall I leave you to speak to him alone?"

"No, no," she cried in a hoarse whisper, instead of her former high-pitched querulous tone. "I cannot—I dare not speak to him alone."

"If forgiveness is needed for the past, Mrs. Mallow," said Luke, in a grave, calm voice, for he had now mastered his emotion, "you have mine freely given, and with it my true sympathy for your position."

She burst into a passionate fit of weeping, which lasted some minutes, during which she stood hiding her face on her uncle's breast; then, recovering herself, she hastily wiped away her tears, and drawing herself up, stood holding out her hand for Luke to take.

He hesitated for a moment, and then, stepping forward, took it and raised it to his lips, just touching it with grave respect, and then letting it fall.

"I wished to say to you, Mr. Ross, let the past be as it were dead, all save our boy and girlhood's days."

"It shall be as you wish," he said, softly.

"You do not bear malice against me?"

"None whatever; but is not this better left,

Mrs. Mallow? Why should we refer so to the past?"

"Because," she said, "I am so alone now, so wanting in help. You have become a great and famous man, whose word is listened to with respect and awe."

"This is folly," he said.

"Folly? Did I not see judge, jury, counsellors hanging upon your lips? did not your words condemn my poor husband this dreadful day?"

"I am afraid, Mrs. Mallow," he said, sadly, "that it needed no advocate's words to condemn your unhappy husband. I would gladly have avoided the task that was, to me, a terrible one; but my word was passed, as a professional man, before I knew whom I had to prosecute. Speaking now, solely from my knowledge of such matters, I am obliged to tell you that nothing could have saved him."

"Hush! Pray do not speak to me like that," she cried. "He is my husband. I cannot—I will not think that he could do so great a wrong."

"Far be it from me," said Luke, gently, "to

try and persuade you to think ill of him.   I should think ill of you, Sage," he added, very softly, " if you fell away from your husband in his sore distress."

" Heaven bless you for those words, Luke Ross !" she cried, as she caught one of his hands and kissed it.   " God will reward you for what you have done in coming to me now, wretched woman that I am, a miserable convict's wife ; but you will help me, will you not ? "

" In any way," he said, earnestly.

She uttered a low sigh of relief, and stood with one hand pressed upon her side, the other upon her brow, as if thinking ; while Portlock sat down by the fire, and, resting his elbows upon his knees, gazed thoughtfully at the warm glow, but intent the while upon what was going on.

" My uncle is very good to me," said Sage, at length, "and is ready to find me what money is required for the object I have in hand ; but I can only obtain paid service, whereas I want the help of one who will work for me as a friend."

She looked at him to see the effect of her words.

Luke bowed his head sadly.

" I want one who, for the sake of the past," she continued, speaking excitedly, "and on account of his generous forgiveness of my cruelty and want of faith, will strain every nerve in my behalf."

She paused again, unable to continue, though fighting vainly to find words.

" I think I understand you," he replied. " You want me, on the strength of the legal knowledge you credit me with, to make some new effort on your husband's behalf ? "

" It is like madness to ask it," she said, " and I tremble as I say the words to you whom he so injured ; but, Luke, have pity on me. He is my husband," she cried, piteously, as she wrung her hands, and then, before he could stay her, flung herself upon the carpet, and clung to his knees. " He is the father of my innocent children ; for God's sake try and save him from this cruel fate."

He remained silent, gazing down at the prostrate figure, as, after an effort or two on his part to raise her, she refused to quit her grovelling attitude, save only to shrink lower, and lay her cheek against his feet.

"Mrs. Mallow!" he said, at last.

"No, no!" she cried, passionately. "Call me Sage again. You have forgiven the past."

"Sage Mallow!" he said, in a low, measured voice.

"You are going to retract your words," she cried, frantically, as she started up. "You are going to draw back."

"I have promised you," he said, quietly, "and my hands, my thoughts, all I possess, are at your service."

"And you will save him?" she cried, joyously.

He remained silent.

"You will work for him—you will forgive him, and bring him back to me?" she cried, piteously. "Luke—Luke Ross—you will save him from this fate?"

"I did not seek this interview," he said, sadly. "Mrs. Mallow, I would have spared you this."

"What do you mean?" she cried. "Will you not try?"

"It would be an act of cruelty," replied Luke, "to attempt to buoy you up with promises that must crumble to the earth."

"You will not try," she cried, passionately.

"I will try. I will try every plan I can think of to obtain your husband's release, Mrs. Mallow," said Luke, gravely.

"Or get him a new trial?"

"Such a thing is impossible. The most we dare hope for would be some slight shortening of his sentence; but candour compels me to say that nothing I can do will be of the slightest avail after such a trial as Cyril Mallow has had."

Just then the old Churchwarden had thoughtfully raised the poker and broken a lump of coal, with the result that the confined gas burst into a bright light, filling the room with its cheerful glow, and Luke saw that Sage was looking at him with flashing eyes, and a couple of scarlet patches were burning in her cheeks.

She raised one hand slowly, and pointed to

the door, speaking in a deep husky voice, full of suppressed passion.

"And I believed in you," she said, wildly, " I thought you would be my friend. I said to myself, Luke Ross is true and noble, and good, and he loved me very dearly, when I was too weak and foolish to realize the value of this love. I said I would beg of you to come to me and help me in my sore distress, that I would humble myself to you, and that in the nobleness of your heart you would forgive the past."

"As I have forgiven it, heaven knows," he said, gravely.

"And then," she cried, excitedly, "you come with your lips full of promises, your heart full of gall, ready to cheer me with words of hope, but only to fall away and leave me in despair."

"Do not misjudge me," he said, appealingly.

"Misjudge you!" she cried, with bitter contempt. "How could I misjudge such a man as you? I see now how false you can be. I see how you laid calmly in wait all these years that you might have revenge. You hurled my poor husband to the earth that afternoon in the lane; now you have crushed him down beneath your heel."

"Can you not be just?" he said.

"Just?" she cried, "to you? I thought to teach my children to bless and reverence your name as that of the man who had saved their father. I taught them to pray for you with their innocent little lips, and I sent to you and humbled myself to ask you to defend my husband in his sore need, but you refused—refused forsooth, because you were gloating over the opportunity you would have for revenge. The trial came, he was condemned through your words, but I still believed you honest, and trusted in you for help. I sent to you once again to pray you to try and restore my husband to me, but you coldly refuse, while your lips are yet hot with promises and lies."

"Sage," he cried, passionately. "you tear my heart."

"I would tear it," she cried, fiercely, in her excitement, "coward that you are — cruel coward, full of deceit and revenge. Go: leave me, let me never see you again, for I could not look upon you without loathing, and I shudder now to think that I have ever touched your hands."

"Sage, my girl, Sage!" said the Church-warden, as he rose and took her hands, "this is madness, and to-morrow you will be sorry for what you have said."

"Uncle." she cried wildly, as she clung to him. "I cannot bear his presence here. Send him from me, or I shall die."

She hid her face upon her uncle's shoulder, and he held out his right hand, and grasped that of Luke.

"God bless you, my boy!" he said, with trembling voice. "She is beside herself with grief, and knows not what she says."

Luke returned the warm pressure of the old farmer's hand, and would have gone, but Portlock held it still.

"I thank you for coming. Luke Ross," he said; "and I know you to be just and true. Would to heaven I had never made that great mistake!"

He said no more. but loosed their visitor's

hand, Luke standing gazing sadly at the sobbing woman for a few moments, and then leaving the room to seek old Michael, with whom he was soon on his way back to chambers, faint and sick at heart.

Hardly had the sound of his footsteps passed from the stairs than, with a wild cry, Sage threw herself upon her knees, sobbing wildly.

"Heaven forgive me!" she cried. "What have I said? Uncle, uncle, a lying spirit has entered into my heart, making me revile him as I have—Luke—so generous, and good, and true."

CHAPTER IX.

BACK HOME.

In obedience to his promise, Luke Ross set earnestly to work to try and obtain an alleviation of the stern sentence passed upon Cyril Mallow.

It was an exceedingly awkward task to come from the prosecuting counsel, but Luke did not shrink, striving with all his might, offending several people high in position by his perseverance, and doing himself no little injury; but he strove on, with the inevitable result that his application came back from the Home Office with the information that the Right Honourable the Secretary of State saw nothing in the sentence to make him interfere with the just course of the law, adding, moreover, his opinion that it was a very proper

punishment for one whose education and ante-
cedents should have guided him to a better
course.

These documents were sent by Luke, without
word of comment, to Kilby Farm, where he
knew from his father that Sage was residing
with her children; and by return of post came
a very brief letter from the widowed wife,
thanking him for what he had done, and
ending with the hope that he would forgive
the words uttered during an agony of soul
that without some utterance would have
driven the speaker mad.

"She did not mean it," said Luke, sadly, as
he carefully folded and put away the letter.
"She knows me better in her heart."

Then time went on, till a year had passed.
Luke had not been near Lawford, for the place,
in spite of its being the home of his birth, was
too full of sad memories to induce him to
go down. Besides, there was the fact that
Sage Mallow had, in defiance of looks askance
from those who had known her in her earlier
days, permanently taken up her residence
there.

"I'd like to hear any one say a slighting word to thee, my bairn," said Portlock, fiercely. "It's no fault of thine that thy husband got into trouble. I'd live here, if it was only out of defiance to the kind-hearted Christians, as they call themselves, who slight thee."

So Sage remained a fixture at the farm, settling down quite into her former life, but no longer with the light elasticity of step, and the rooms no more echoed with the ring of her musical voice. Time had given her an older and a sadder look, but her features had grown refined, and there was a ladylike mien in every movement that made her aunt gaze upon her with a kind of awe.

"Let her come back to the old nest again, mother," said Portlock. "There's room enough for the lass, and as for the little ones— My word, mother, it's almost like being grand-father and granny."

Many a heartache had Sage had about her dependent position, and the heavy losses that had occurred to her uncle in the money she and her husband had had; but Portlock, in his bluff way, made light of it.

"I dare say I can make some more, my bairn, and it will do for these two young tyrants. Hang me, what a slave they do make of me, to be sure!"

It was the faint wintry sunshine of Sage Mallow's life to see the newly-born love of the old people for her children, whom they idolized, and great was the jealousy of Rue whenever she came across to Kilby. But it was no wonder, for they were as attractive in appearance as they were pretty in their ways. One was always out in the gig with the Churchwarden, while the other was seriously devoting herself to domestic duties and hindering Mrs. Portlock, who bore the infliction with huge delight.

"I never saw such bairns," cried the old lady.

"Nor anybody else," said Portlock, proudly. "Let's see, mother, there's a year gone by out of the fourteen. Bless my soul, I wish it had been twenty-one instead."

"For shame, Joseph!" cried Mrs. Portlock. "How can you!"

"Well, all I can say is that it's a blessing

he was shut up where he could do no further mischief."

" But it's so dreadful for the bairns."

" Tchah ! not it. They can't help it, bless 'em. See how they've improved since they have been down here."

" Well, yes, they have," said Mrs. Portlock, " and Sage's a deal better."

" Better, poor lassie ! I should think she is. Of course, she frets after him a bit now and then, and feels the disgrace a good deal, but, bless my soul, mother, she's like a new woman compared to what she was. For my part, I hope they'll never let him out again."

" For shame, Joseph !" said Mrs. Portlock. " Mr. Mallow was over here this morning."

" Was he ? Ah, I'll be bound to say he wanted to take the bairns over to the rectory."

" Yes, and he took them."

" Hah !" said the farmer, sharply. " I'm very sorry for the poor old lady, but I am glad that she is so ill that she can't bear to have them much."

" What a shame, Joseph !" cried Mrs. Portlock, indignantly. "How can you say such a cruel thing! Glad she is so ill!"

"I didn't mean I was glad she was ill," said the Churchwarden, chuckling. "I meant I was glad she was too ill to have the bairns."

"But it sounds so dreadful."

"Let it. What do I care! I don't want for us to be always squabbling over those children. They're my Sage's bairns, and consequently they're ours."

"But they're Cyril Mal——"

"Tchah! Don't mention his name," cried the Churchwarden.

"Fie, Joseph! you do make me jump so when you talk like that."

"Shouldn't mention that fellow's name then. I told you not."

"Well, then, they are Mr. and Mrs. Mallow's children just as much as ours, Joseph," said the old lady.

"No they ain't; they're mine, and there's an end of it. I say, though, old Michael Ross is ill."

"Ah! poor man. I'm sorry; but he's very old, Joseph."

"Not he. Young man yet," said the Church-warden, who was getting touchy on the score of age. "I don't call a man old this side of a hundred: Look at the old chaps in the Bible, as Sammy Warmoth used to say."

"Yes, Joseph, but they were great and good men."

"Oh, were they?" said the Churchwarden. "I don't know so much about that. Some of 'em were; but others did things that the Lawford people wouldn't stand if I were to try 'em on."

"But what is the matter with Michael Ross?"

"Break up. I went in to see him, and the old man got me to write a letter to Luke, asking him to come down and see him."

"And did you, Joseph?"

"Did I? Why, of course I did. Do you suppose I've got iron bowels, woman, and no compassion in me at all?"

"I wish you wouldn't talk such nonsense, Joseph," said Mrs. Portlock, sharply. "And do you think Luke Ross will come down?"

"Of course he will."

"He hasn't been down for a very long time now. I suppose he has grown to be such a great man that he is ashamed of poor old Lawford."

"Who's talking nonsense now?" cried the Churchwarden. "Nice temptation there is for him to come down here, isn't there? Bless the lad, I wonder he even cares to set foot in the place again."

"It would be unpleasant for him, I suppose, after all that has taken place. But you think he will come?"

"Sure to. I told him it was urgent, and that I'd drive over to Morbro and meet the train, so as to save him time. He's a good man, is Luke Ross, as old Michael said with tears in his eyes to-day, and he wants to see him badly."

"Poor old man!"

"Tchah! don't call him old," cried the Churchwarden. Then calming down after a whiff or two of his pipe, "Luke Ross will be down here to-morrow afternoon as sure as a gun. Eh? Why, Sage, my gal, I didn't see you there"

" Did—did I hear you aright, uncle ? " she said, faintly. " Is old Mr. Ross ill ? "

" Very ill, my dear," said the Churchwarden, sternly, " and Luke Ross is coming down to see him, I should say."

CHAPTER X.

DOWN AT LAWFORD.

PORTLOCK was right in saying that Luke would be down the next day, for, reproaching himself for his neglect of his father, he hastened down to find him somewhat recovered from the sudden attack that had prostrated him, and the old man's face lit up as his son entered the room.

"Yes, my boy, better; yes, I'm better," he said, feebly; "but it can't be for long, Luke; it can't be for long. I'm very, very glad you have come."

"But you are better," said Luke; "and good spirits have so much to do with recovery."

"Well, yes, my boy, yes," said the old man; "and the sight of you again seems to have given me strength.　You won't go back again yet, Luke?"

"I was going back to-morrow, father," he said; "but," he added, on seeing the look of disappointment in the old man's face, "I will stay a little longer."

"Do, my boy, do," cried the old man; "and when I go off to sleep, as I shall soon—I sleep a great deal now, my boy—go and look round, and say a word to our neighbours.　I often talk to them about you, Luke, and tell them that though you have grown to be a great man you are not a bit proud, and I should like them to see that you are not."

"That is soon done," said Luke, laughing. "Why should I be proud?"

"Oh, you might be, my boy, but you are not.　Go and have a chat with Tomlinson and Fullerton.　And, Luke, if you wouldn't mind, when you are that way, I'd go in and see Humphrey Bone."

"Is he still master?" said Luke, thoughtfully, as the old days came vividly back.

"No, my boy, not for these two years; and he's quite laid by.　An old man before his

time, Luke, and it is the drink that has done
it. I don't judge him hardly though, for we
never know what another's weakness has been,
and it is not for us to sit in judgment upon
our brother's faults. Will you go and see him,
Luke ?"

" I will, father," said the younger man, smiling and feeling refreshed, after his arduous
daily toil and study of man's greed, rapacity,
and sin, with the simple, innocent kindness of
his father's heart.

"That does me good, my boy, indeed it
does," said the old man, pathetically; and
he held his son's hand against his true old
breast. "I'm very sorry for a great deal
that I have done, my boy, and I like to see
you growing up free from many of the weak-
nesses and hard ways that have been mine.
What I am obliged to leave undone, Luke, I
want you to do, for my time is very short, and
I often lie here and think that I should like to
go before the Master feeling that I had tried to
do my best, and taught you, my boy, according
to such knowledge of good as in me lay."

" My dear old father !" cried Luke, tenderly ;

and the hard, worldly crust that was gathering upon him seemed to melt away as he leaned over and carefully smoothed and turned the old man's pillow with all the gentleness of a woman's hand. "Why, what is it?" he said, as the old man uttered quite a sob, and the weak tears gathered in his eyes.

"Nothing, my boy, it is nothing," he said. " It only made me think of thirty years ago, when I was ill, and your mother used to turn my pillow like that—just like that, my boy— and you are so much like her, Luke; and as I lie here, a worn-out, trembling old man, and you come down—you, my boy, who have grown so great, and who, they tell me, will some day be Queen's Counsel, and perhaps Attorney-General, and then a Judge, such a great man as you've become, Luke—I lie here thinking that you can come down and tend to me like this, it makes me thank God that I have such a son."

" Why, what have I done more than any other son would do? And as to becoming great, what nonsense ! "

" But it isn't nonsense, Luke, my boy,"

quavered the old man. "I've heard all about it: and, Luke, when you are Queen's Counsel, my boy, give her good advice, for kings and queens have much to answer for, and I should like her—God bless her!—to have a very long and happy reign."

"Indeed I will, father," said Luke, laughing, "if ever it falls to my lot to be her adviser. But there, you are getting too much excited. Suppose you try and have a nap?"

"I will, my boy, I will, and you'll go round town a bit, and walk up and see the parson. He'll be strange and glad to see thee, and if you see Mrs. Cyril, say a kind word to the poor soul; she's been very good to me, my boy, and comes and sits and talks to me a deal. Don't think about the past, my boy, but about the future. Let's try and do all the kindness we can, Luke, while we are here. Life is very short, my boy—a very, very little span."

"Father," said Luke, bending over the old man's pillow, "for your sake and your kindly words, I'll do the best I can."

"Thank you, my boy, God bless you, I know you will," said the old man. "For life is so short, Luke, my son. Good-bye, my boy. Do all the good you can. I'm going to sleep now. God bless you. good-bye."

He closed his eyes, and drew a long breath, dropping off at once into a calm and restful slumber, Luke staying by his side for a while.

Then taking out a blue official-looking document from his pocket, he looked at it for a few moments before replacing it in his breast.

"Poor old man!" he said, softly. "I wish I had told him what I was about to do, it would have pleased him to know."

He got up and went softly down-stairs, to pause for a few minutes in the homely, comfortably furnished room with its well-polished furniture, every knob and handle seeming like familiar friends. There was his father's seat. his mother's, and the little windsor arm-chair that had been his own, religiously preserved, and kept as bright as beeswax and sturdy country hands could make it.

"He has gone off to sleep," Luke said to the matronly housekeeper, who never ventured to speak to him without a curtsey.

"No, Mr. Luke, sir—I mean yes, Mr. Luke,

sir, I'll keep going up and peeping at him, and take him his beef tea when he wackens. Your coming, sir, begging your pardon for taking the liberty of saying so, sir, have done him a power of good."

Luke smiled and nodded—"so condescending and kind-like," the woman afterwards told a neighbour—and walked out across the market-place, stopping to shake hands here and there with the tradesmen who came to their doors, and at last making his way down towards the schools.

"They seem to esteem me a very great gun," he said, half in jest, half bitterly, as he walked slowly on, passing men whom he remembered as boys, and responding constantly to the salutations he received.

He had not intended to go that way, thinking he would send his missive over to Kilby by post, and asking himself why he had not mentioned the matter to Portlock as he drove him in that day; but somehow his footsteps turned in the direction of the farm, and he had nearly reached the turning indelibly marked in his memory as the one along which he had come that cruel eve, when suddenly a merry shout from a childish voice fell upon his ear.

He did not know why it should, but it seemed to thrill him as he went on, to come in sight of two bright, golden-haired little girls, each with her pinky fingers full of flowers, and her chubby face flushed with exercise.

They stopped and gazed at him for a moment, and then ran back.

"I'm not one whom young folks take to," he said, bitterly; and then his heart seemed to stand still, for he saw them run up to a pale, graceful-looking woman, who bent down, and evidently said something to the children, both of whom hesitated for a moment, and then came running back.

"Sage," he said to himself, as he involuntarily stopped short. "How changed!"

Then, as he saw the children approach, an involuntary feeling of repugnance came over him, and his heart seemed to shrink from the encounter.

His children. So pretty, but with a something in their innocent faces that reminded him terribly of their father.

He would have turned back, but he was spell-bound, and the next moment the little things were at his side, the elder to take his hand and kiss it, saying in her silvery, childish voice —

"I can't reach to kiss you more, for being so good to poor mamma."

"And I'll dive you my fowers, Mitter Luke," said the other little thing. "Sagey pick all hertelf."

An agony of shame, of love, of regret and pleasure commingled seemed to sweep across Luke Ross, as, with convulsed face, he went down on one knee in the road and caught the little ones to his breast.

"My darlings!" he cried, hoarsely, as he kissed them passionately.

Then, with his eyes blinded by the hot tears of agony, he caught the blue envelope from his breast and pressed it into the youngest little one's hands.

"Take it to mamma, my child, and say Luke Ross prays that it may make her happy."

Then, unable to command his feelings, he turned and walked away.

CHAPTER XI.

LUKE VISITS AN OLD FRIEND.

" LIFE is very short, my boy, a very little span," seemed to keep repeating itself to Luke Ross's ears, as he walked briskly across the fields trying to regain his composure, hardly realizing that he was going in the direction of the rectory, till he had nearly reached the gates, when he paused, not daring to enter.

" It would be almost an insult after the part I was forced to play," he said to himself, and he set off towards the town.

But somehow his father's words seemed to keep repeating themselves, and he altered his mind, turned back, and went in.

" I go in all kindliness," he said to himself;

" and perhaps the poor old man would like to know what I have done."

The next minute he stopped short, hardly recognizing in the bent, pallid figure, with snowy hair, the fine, portly Rector of a dozen years ago.

" I beg your pardon ; my sight is not so good as it was," said the old man apologetically, as he shaded his eyes with a hand holding a trowel.

" It is Luke Ross, Mr. Mallow. I was down here for the first time for some years, and I thought I would call."

The old man neither moved nor spoke for a few moments, but stood as if turned to stone.

Then recovering himself, but still terribly agitated by the recollections that the meeting brought up, he held out his hand.

" I am glad you came, Luke, very glad," he said. " I—I call you Luke," he continued, smiling, " it seems so familiar. Your visit, my boy, honours me, and I am very, very glad you came."

There was a thoroughly genial warmth in the old man's greeting as he passed his arm through that of his visitor, and led him into one of the glass-houses that it was his joy to tend.

"I hear a good deal about you, Mr. Ross, and go and chat with your father about you. But—but, my boy, you have seen him, have you not?"

"I was with him till he went to sleep, not an hour ago."

"That is well, that is well," said the Rector, who had fallen into the old life habit of repeating himself. "Stay with him awhile if you can, Luke. Life is very uncertain at his age, and I have my fears about him—grave fears indeed."

"He is a great age, Mr. Mallow," said Luke, "but he quite cheered up when I came."

"He would," said the Rector, with his voice trembling, "he would, Luke Ross, and—and I cannot help feeling how hard is my own lot compared to his. Luke Ross," he said, after an effort to recover his calmness, "I have no son to be a blessing to me in my old age; three of my children have quite passed away."

It seemed no time for words, and Luke felt

that the greatest kindness on his part would be to hold his peace.

The old Rector appeared to recover from his emotion soon after, as Luke asked after Mrs. Mallow.

"It would be foolish," said the Rector, "if I said not well. Poor thing; she is a sad invalid, but she bears it with exemplary patience, Luke Ross. See," he continued. pointing to a waxy-looking, sweet-scented flower, "this is a plant I am trying to cultivate for her. She is so fond of flowers. It is hard work to get it to grow though. It requires heat, and I find it difficult to keep it at the right temperature."

Luke kept hoping that the old man would make some fresh allusion to his son, and give an opportunity for introducing something the visitor wished to say.

"I grow a great many grapes now," continued the Rector, "and I have so arranged my houses that I have grapes from June right up to March."

"Indeed, sir," said Luke, as he noted more and more how the old man had changed. He had become garrulous, and prattled on with rather a vacant smile upon his lip, as he led his visitor from place to place, pointing out the various objects in which he took pride.

For a time Luke felt repelled by the old man's weakness, but as he found that one idea ran through all this conversation, a sweet, tender devotion for the suffering wife, respect took the place of the approach to contempt.

"You will not mind, Luke Ross," he said, "if I stop to cut a bunch of grapes for my poor wife, will you?"

"Indeed, no, sir," said Luke, narrowly watching him.

"She does not know that I have one in such a state of perfection," he said, laughing, "for I've kept it a secret. Poor soul! she is so fond of grapes; and, do you know, Luke Ross, I'm quite convinced that there is a great deal of nutriment and support in this fruit, for sometimes when my poor darling cannot touch food of an ordinary kind she will go on enjoying grapes, and they seem to support. and keep her alive."

"It is very probable that it is as you say, sir."

"Yes, I think it is," said the old Rector. slowly drawing forward a pair of steps, and planting them just beneath where a large bunch of grapes hung, beautifully covered with violet bloom. "There," he said, taking a pair of pocket scissors from his vest. and opening them. "Look at that, Luke Ross. eh! Isn't that fine?"

"As fine as we see in Covent-garden, sir."

"That they are. that they are, and I grow them entirely myself, Luke Ross. Nobody touches them but me. I dress and prune my vines myself, and thin the bunches. No other hand touches them but mine. Now for a basket."

He took a pretty little wicker basket from a nail whereon it hung, and then, with a pleasant smile upon his face, he snipped off half-a-dozen leaves, which he carefully arranged in the bottom of the basket, so as to form a bed for the bunch of grapes.

"So much depends upon the appearance of anything for an invalid. Luke Ross." he said, smiling with pleasure as he went on. "I have to make things look very attractive sometimes if I want her to eat. Now, then, I think that we shall do."

"Shall I cut the bunch for you, Mr. Mallow?" said Luke, as he saw, with a feeling of apprehension, that the old man was about to mount the frail steps.

"Cut—cut the bunch?" said the Rector, looking at him aghast. "Oh, dear no; I could not let any one touch them but myself. No—no disrespect, my young friend," he said, apologetically, "but she is very weak, and I have to tempt her to eat. My dear boy—I mean my dear Mr. Ross—if she thought that any hand had touched them but mine she would not eat them; and it is by these little things that I have been able to keep her alive so long."

He sat down on the top of the steps as he spoke, and smiled blandly from his throne.

"You will not feel hurt, Mr. Ross?" he said, gently. "I appreciate your kindness. You are afraid that I shall fall, but I am very cautious. See how much time I take."

He smiled pleasantly as he went on with his task, rising carefully, taking tightly hold of the stout wires that supported the vine, and steadying himself on the top of the steps till he felt quite safe, when, letting go his hold, he placed the basket tenderly beneath the perfect bunch of grapes, raising it a little till the fruit lay in the bed of leaves prepared for its repose, and then there was a sharp snip of the scissors at the stalk, and the old man looked down with a sort of serene joy in his countenance.

"Are they not lovely?" he said, as he carefully descended, until he stood in safety upon the red-brick floor.

He held up the basket of violet-bloomed berries for his visitor to see, smiling with pleasure as he saw the openly-displayed admiration for the beautiful fruit.

"They make her so happy," said the old man, with tears standing in his eyes. "Don't think me weak, Mr. Ross. It is a sad thing. all these many years, sir, to be confined to her couch, helpless, and dependent on those who love her," said the old man, again dreamily. as he gazed down at the grapes.

"Think you weak, Mr. Mallow?" cried

Luke, with energy. "No, sir; I thank God that we have such men as you on earth."

The old man shook his head sadly.

"No, no—no, no," he said. "A weak, foolish, indulgent man, Mr. Ross, whom his Master will weigh in the balance and find wanting. But I have tried to do my best—weakly, Mr. Ross, but weakly. I fear that my trumpet has given forth but an uncertain sound."

Just then an idea seemed to strike the old man, who smiled pleasantly, set his basket down, took another from a nail, and then snipped more leaves, and gazed up at his bunches for a few moments, his handsome old face being a study as his eyes wandered from cane to cane.

Suddenly his face lit up more and more, and he turned to Luke.

"You shall move the steps for me," he said. "Just there, under that large bunch."

Luke obeyed, wondering, and the old man then handed him the basket and scissors.

"You shall cut that bunch for me, Mr. Ross, please."

"Really, sir,——" began Luke.

"Please oblige me, Mr. Ross. You saw how I did it. I will hold the steps; you shall not fall."

Luke smiled as he thought of the risk; and then, to humour the old man, he mounted, the Rector watching him intently.

"You will be very careful, Mr. Ross," he said. "Let the bunch glide, as it were, into the leaves. A little more to the right. Now then cut—cut!"

The scissors gave a sharp snip, and the second bunch reclined in its green bed.

"I didn't think of it before," said the Rector, whose face glowed with pleasure as Luke descended. "They are not quite so fine as this bunch," he said, apologetically.

"Really, I hardly see any difference, Mr. Mallow," replied Luke.

"Very little, Luke Ross. Will you carry them home with you? Your father will be pleased with them, I know. He likes my grapes, Mr. Ross."

Luke's answer was to grasp the old man's hand, which he retained as he spoke.

"I thank you, Mr. Mallow," he said. "It

was thoughtful and kind of you to the poor old man. Now, may I say something to you? Forgive me if I bring up painful things."

"It is something about Julia, or about my son," gasped the Rector. "Tell me quickly— tell me the worst."

"Be calm, Mr. Mallow," said Luke, quietly; "there is nothing wrong."

"Thank God!" said the old man, fervently, with a sigh that was almost a groan. "Thank God!"

"After some difficulty and long trying, I obtained a permit for two visitors to see Cyril Mallow at Peatmoor, and that permit I have placed this afternoon in Mrs. Cyril's hands."

"Permission—to see my son?" faltered the old man.

"Yes, sir. I thought that you would accompany your daughter-in-law to see him."

The old man stood with his hands clasped, gazing sadly in his visitor's face, but without speaking.

At last he shook his head sadly.

"No," he said, "I cannot go. I should

dread the meeting. I think it would kill me, Luke. But if it were my duty, I would go. I have one here, though—one I cannot neglect. It would take three or four days, at least, to go and return. I could not leave my dear wife as many hours, or I should return and find her dead. Go for me, Luke. Take that poor, suffering woman, and let her see him once again."

"I—I take her?" cried Luke, starting. "Mr. Mallow!"

"It would be an act of gentle charity," said the old man, "and I would bless you for your love. But I must go now, Luke Ross," he said, half vacantly. "My head is very weak now. I am old, and I have had much trouble. You will give your father the grapes—with my love?"

He took up his own basket, and the sight of the soft violet fruit appeared to soothe him, for he began to smile pleasantly, seeming quite to have forgotten the allusion to the permit; and in this spirit he walked with Luke to the gate, shook hands almost affectionately, and they parted.

CHAPTER XII.

A LONG SLEEP.

IF the Rector was placid and calm once more, so was not Luke Ross, whose pulses still throbbed more heavily than was their wont, as he thought of the old man's words, and then, as it were to weave itself in with them, came the recollection of that which his father had said—that life was very short, and begging him to do all the good he could.

"It is impossible," he cried at last. "I, too, could not bear it."

He strode onward, walking more rapidly, for a strange feeling of dread oppressed him, and as he seemed to keep fighting against the possibility of his acceding to the Rector's request, the words of the weak old man he had left asleep kept recurring, bidding him try to do all the good he could, for life was so very short.

"But he will forget by to-morrow that he asked me," said Luke, half aloud. "It is a mad idea, and I could not go."

As he reached the town, first one and then another familiar face appeared, and more than one of their owners seemed disposed to stop and speak, but Luke was too preoccupied, and he hurried on to his old home to find the housekeeper waiting for him at the door.

"How is he?" he cried, quickly, for his conscience smote him for being so long away.

"Sleeping as gently as a baby, sir," the woman said. "Oh, what lovely grapes, sir. He will be so pleased with them. The doctor came in soon after you had gone out, and went and looked at him, but he said he was not to be disturbed on any account, so that he has not had his beef-tea."

Luke found the table spread for his benefit as he crossed the room to go gently up-stairs and bend over the bed, where, as the housekeeper had said, old Michael Ross was sleeping as calmly as an infant. So Luke stole down once more to partake of the substantial meal prepared on his special behalf, the housekeeper refusing to seat herself at the same table with him.

"No, sir," she said, stiffly, "I know my duty to my betters too well for that. Michael Ross is an old neighbour, and knew my master well before he died, poor man."

"Do you think one of us ought to sit with my father?" said Luke, quickly, as the woman's last words seemed to raise up a fresh train of troublous thought.

"I'll go and sit with him, sir, if you like," said the woman, "but both doors are open, and the ceiling is so thin that you can almost hear him breathe."

"Perhaps it is not necessary," said Luke, quickly. "You'll excuse my being anxious."

"As if I didn't respect you the more for it, Mr. Luke, sir," said the woman, warmly; "but as I was saying, I always had my meals with your dear father, sir."

"Then why not sit down here?"

"Because things have changed, sir. We all

know how you have got to be a famous man, and are rising still, sir; and we are proud of what you've done, and so I'd rather wait upon you, if you please."

Luke partook of his meal mechanically, listening the while for any sound from up-stairs, and twice over he rose and went up to find that the sleep was perfectly undisturbed.

Then he reseated himself, and went on dreamily, thinking of the old man's words.

" Life is very short, my boy. Do all the good you can."

Over and over again he kept on repeating old Michael's words, when they were not, with endless variations, repeating themselves.

Then came the possibility of his going down with Sage to see Cyril Mallow.

" No; it is impossible," he said again. " Why should I go? What right have I there? I cannot—I will not—go."

He rose, and went up-stairs to rest himself by the old man's bed, finding that he had not moved; and here Luke sat, thinking of the past, of the change from busy London, his chambers, and the briefs he had to read.

Then he went back again in the past, seeming to see in the darkness of the room, partly illumined by a little shaded lamp, the whole of his past career, till a feeling of anger seemed to rise once more against Cyril Mallow, against Sage, and the fate that had treated him so ill.

Just then the housekeeper came up and looked at the old man, nodding softly, as if to say, "He is all right," and then she stole out again on tiptoe.

Again the interweaving thoughts kept forming strange patterns before the watcher's eyes, as hour after hour calmly glided by till close on midnight. Misery, despair, disappointment, seemed to pervade Luke's brain, to the exclusion of all thought of his great success, and the troubles that must fall into each life, and then came a feeling of calm and repose, as he thought once more of the words of the patient old man beside whose bed he was seated.

"I'll try, father," he suddenly said, "I'll try. Self shall be forgotten, for the sake of my promises to you."

He had risen with the intention of going down on his knees by the old man's bed, when the housekeeper entered the room.

"I've brought you a cup of tea, sir," she whispered. "It's just on the stroke of two, sir, and I thought if you'd go to bed now I'd sit up with him."

"I mean to sit up with him to-night," said Luke, quietly; "but ought he to sleep so long as this at once?"

"Old people often do, sir, and it does 'em good. If you lean over him, sir, you can hear how softly he is a breath—— Oh, Mr. Luke, sir!"

"Quick! the doctor," cried Luke, excitedly. "No; I'll go," and he rushed to the door.

There was no need, for old Michael Ross was fast asleep—sleeping as peacefully and well as those sleep who calmly drop into the gentle rest prepared for the weary when the fulness of time has come.

CHAPTER XIII.

SOUNDS IN THE FOG.

A WEEK had passed since old Michael Ross had been conveyed to his final resting-place, followed by all the tradesmen of the place, and a goodly gathering beside, for in the Woldshire towns a neighbour is looked upon as a neighbour indeed. While he lives he may be severely criticised, perhaps hardly dealt with; but come sickness or sorrow, willing hands are always ready with assistance; and when the saddest trial of all has passed, there is always a display of general sympathy for the bereft.

On this occasion pretty well every shop was closed and blind drawn down.

And now the quaint country funeral was past, the cakes had been eaten, and after seeing, as well as he could, to his father's affairs, Luke had said his farewells to those who were only too eager to manifest their hearty goodwill.

The vehicle that was to take him to the station was waiting at his door, and he stepped in with his portmanteau, Portlock being the driver; and then, with a rattle of hoofs and a whirr of wheels, they crossed the market-place, followed by a hearty cheer, while at door after door as they passed there were townspeople waving hands and kerchiefs, till the dog-cart was out of sight.

Luke could not help feeling moved at the manifestations of friendliness, though, at the same time, he smiled, and thought of how strange these quaint, old-style ways of the people, far removed from the civilizing influence of the railway, seemed to him after his long sojourn in the metropolis.

As he thought, he recalled the solemn processions of hearses and mourning coaches, with velvet and plumes, and trampling black, long-tailed horses, common in London; and in his then mood he could not help comparing them with the funeral of the week before, when six of his fellow-townsmen lifted old Michael Ross's coffin by the handles, and bore it between them, hanging at arm's length, through the town, with the church choir, headed by their leader, singing a funeral hymn.

There seemed something far more touching and appealing to the senses in these simple old country ways; and as Luke Ross pondered on them his spirit was very low.

The Churchwarden respected his silence, and did not speak save to his horse, a powerful beast that trotted sharply; and so they went on till Luke was roused from his reverie by the sudden check by the roadside.

He might have been prepared for it if he had given the matter a thought, but he had been too much wrapped up in his troubles to think that if they were to pick up Mrs. Cyril Mallow on the road it would probably be at the end of this lane.

It came to him now, though, like a shock, as Portlock drew rein, and Luke recalled like a flash how, all those years ago, he had leaped down from the coach light-hearted and eager, to follow the course of the lane, picking the scattered wild flowers as he went, till he came upon the scene which seemed to blast his future life.

But there was no time for further thought, and he drove away these fancies of the past as he leaped down and assisted Sage Mallow, who was waiting closely veiled with her aunt, to mount into the seat beside her uncle, while he took the back.

Then a brief farewell was taken, all present being too full of their own thoughts to speak, and almost in silence they drove over to the county town, where one of the old farmer's men had preceded them with the luggage, and was in waiting to bring back the horse.

It was on a brilliant morning, a couple of days later, that the party of three reached the old West of England city, from whence they would have to hire a fly to take them across to the great prison at Peatmoor. The journey had been made almost in silence, Sage being still closely veiled, and seeming to be constantly striving to hide the terrible emotion from which she suffered.

At such times as they had stopped for refreshment Luke had seemed to have completely set aside the past, treating her with a quiet deference, and attending to her in a gentle, sympathetic way which set her at her ease, while in her heart she thanked him for his kindness.

Their plans had been that Portlock was to be their companion to the prison gates, where he would wait with the fly while Luke escorted the suffering woman within, of course leaving her to meet her husband.

As they drove on with the battered old horse that drew the fly, surmounting slowly the successive hills that had to be passed before they reached the bleak table-land overlooking the far-reaching sea where the prison was placed, Luke Ross could not help thinking how strange it was that, with all around so bright and fair in the morning sun, they alone should be moody and sorrowful of heart. He glanced at the Churchwarden, who returned the gaze, but did not speak, only sank back farther in his corner of the shabby vehicle. He turned his eyes almost involuntarily upon

Sage, but there was no penetrating the thick crape veil she wore, and had he met her gaze, the chances are that he would have felt it better not to speak.

Sage was bearing up bravely, but Luke could see that from time to time some throb of emotion shook her frame, and on one of these occasions he softly opened the door of the fly, and, without stopping the driver, leaped out to walk beside the horse up the steep moorland hill they were ascending.

"Hard work for a horse, zir," said the man; "and these roads are so awful bad. Gove'ment pretends to make 'em wi' convict labour, but the work is never half done."

"They might break the stones a little smaller," said Luke, absently.

"Smaller, zir!" said the driver, as the fly jolted on, "why they arn't broke at all. Fine view here, zir," he said as he stopped 'to let the panting horse get its wind.

"Splendid," said Luke, as he gazed at the wide prospect of moorland and sea. There was scarcely a tree to be seen, but the great expanse was dotted with huge blocks of gray granite, weather-stained, lichened, and worn by centuries of battling with the storm. The prevailing tint was gray, but here and there were gorgeous patches of purple heather, golden broom, and ruddy orange-yellow gorse, with creamy streaks of bog moss, heath pools, and green clumps of water plants glistening in the sun.

On his left was the deep blue sea, dotted with white-sailed yachts and trawlers, with luggers spreading each a couple of cinnamon-red sails, and seeming to lie motionless upon the glassy surface, for the ripple and heave were invisible from the great height at which they were.

"Aye, it's a fine view from up here, zir, and though I don't know much about other counties, I don't s'pose there's many as can beat this."

"It is fine," said Luke, whose thoughts were changed by the brightness of the scene, and the brisk, bracing air sent a thrill of pleasure through his frame.

"They do say, zir, as you can zee a matter of forty mile from a bit higher up yonder on a clear time," continued the man, who appeared glad of a chance to talk; "but we shan't zee that, nor half on it, to-day, zir, for there's a zea-fog coming on, a reg'lar thick one. Look, zir, you can zee it come sweeping along over the zea like zmoke."

"It is curious," said Luke, watching the strange phenomenon, as by degrees it blotted out boat after boat, ship after ship, till it reached the land, and seemed to begin ascending the slopes.

"Much as we shall do to reach the prison, zir, before it's on us," said the man. "You zee it's all up-hill, zir, or we could get on faster."

"But it will not matter, will it?" said Luke, "You know the road?"

"Oh, I know the way well enough, zir, but it comes on zo thick sometimes that all you can do is to get down and lead the horse, feeling like, to keep on the road."

"But they don't last long, I suppose?"

"Half-an-hour zome of 'em, zir, zome an hour, zome for a whole day. There's no telling when a fog comes on how long it's going to be. All depends on the wind, zir."

"They are only inconvenient, these fogs, I suppose?" said Luke, as they went on; "there is nothing else to mind."

"Lor', no, zir, nothing at all if zo be as you've brought a bit o' lunch with you. When I get into a thick one I generally dra' up to the zide of the road and put on the horse's nose-bag, to let him amuse himself while I have a pipe."

"And where does the prison lie now?" said Luke, after a pause.

"That's it, zir," said the man, pointing with his whip, "just where you zee the fog crossing. They'll be in it before us, and p'raps we shall be in it when they're clear. Perhaps you'll get inside, zir, now; I'm going to trot the horse a bit."

"I'll get up beside you," said Luke, quietly; and he took his place by the driver.

"Fine games there is up here zometimes, zir," said the man, who was glad to find a good listener. "The convicts are out in gangs all over the moor, zir, working under the charge of warders. Zome's chipping stone, and zome's making roads; and now and then, zir, when there's a real thick fog, zome of 'em makes a run for it, and no wonder. I should if I had a chance, for they have a hard time of it up there."

"And do they get away?"

"Not often, zir," said the driver, as, with a half-repressed shudder, Luke listened to the man's words, for like a flash they had suggested to him the possibility of Cyril Mallow trying to effect his escape. "You zee the warders look pretty zharp after them, and their orders are strict enough. Once they catch sight of a man running and he won't surrender, they zhoot him down."

"So I have heard."

"Yes, zir, they zhoot un down like as if they were dogs. They're bads uns enough, I dessay, and deserves it, but zomehow it zeems to go again the grain, zir, that it do, to zhoot 'em."

"Then you would not shoot one if you were a warder?" said Luke, hardly knowing what he spoke.

"I wouldn't if I was a zojer, sir. Poor beggars' liberty's sweet, and may be if they got away they'd turn over a new leaf. No, zir, I wouldn't zhoot 'em, and I wouldn't let out to the warders which way a runaway had gone. I'd scorn it," said the man, giving his horse a tremendous lash in his excitement.

"It does seem a cowardly thing to do."

"Cowardly, zir? It's worse," said the man, indignantly. "I call it the trick of a zneak; but the people about here do it fast enough for the zake of the reward."

"There, zir, I told you so," continued the man, after a quarter of an hour's progress, during which he had been pointing out pieces of scenery to inattentive ears. "The fog 'll be on uz in vive minutes more."

They were descending a sharp hill as the man spoke, and in half the time he had named they were in the midst of a dense vapour, so thick that Luke fully realized the necessity for stopping if they wished to avoid an accident.

"I think we can get down here, zir, and across the next bit of valley, and then it will perhaps be clearer as we get higher up. Anyhow we'll try."

Keeping the horse at a walk, he drove cautiously on, finished the descent, went along a level for a short distance, and then they began once more to ascend.

" I'll try it for two or three hundred yards, zir," said the man, "and then if it don't get better we must stop and chance it."

What he meant by chancing it the driver did not explain, but as with every hundred yards they went the fog seemed thicker, he suddenly drew the rein and pulled his horse's nose-bag from beneath the seat.

" If you'll excuse me, zir, I'd get inside if I was you, and wait patiently till the wind springs up. These fogs are very raw and cold, and rheumaticky to strangers, and you arn't got your great-coat on."

" Hush! man, what's that?" said Luke, excitedly, as just then came the dull distant report of some piece.

" Zhooting," said the man, coolly, as he took out the horse's bit and strapped on his nose-bag.

"Do you mean that shot was fired at a convict?" said Luke, hoarsely.

"Safe enough," said the man.

Luke leaped down.

"I think I'd draw up the windows, Mr. Portlock," he said. "The fog is very dank and chilly now."

"Won't you come in?"

"Thanks, no. Draw up the windows. I'll stop and chat with the man. I dare say the mist will soon pass away."

As the windows were drawn up, Luke uttered a sigh of relief, for it was horrible to him that Sage should hear what was going on, and just then there was another report, evidently nearer.

"I thought they'd be at it," said the man. "Mind me smoking, zir?"

"No: go on; but don't speak so loudly. I don't want the lady inside to hear."

"All right, zir. Beg pardon," said the man, lighting his pipe. "They're sure to make a bolt for it on a day like this. Hear that, zir? I hope they won't zhoot this way, for a rifle ball goes a long way zometimes."

"Yes, I heard," said Luke, feeling an unwonted thrill of excitement in his veins. "That shot could not have been far off."

"Half a mile, or maybe a mile, zir," replied the man. "It's very hard to tell in a fog. Zounds is deceiving. There goes another. It's hot to-day, and no mistake."

Just then they heard a distant shout or two answered in another direction, and once more all was still.

"Let's see, zir," said the driver, who stood leaning against his horse, and puffing unconcernedly away, perfectly cool, while Luke's blood seemed rising to fever heat; "it's just about zigs months since that I was driving along here after a fog, and I come along a gang carrying one of their mates on a roughly-made stretcher thing, with half-a-dozen warders with loaded rifles marching un along. The poor chap they was carrying had made a bolt of it, zir, but they had zeen and fired at him; but he kept on, and they didn't find him for three hours after, and then they run right upon him lying by one of the little ztreams. Poor chap. he was bleeding to death, and that makes 'em thirsty, they zay. Anyhow, they found him scooping up the water with his hand, and drinking of it, and as he come up alongside of me he zmiled up at me like, and then he zhut his eyes."

" Did he die ? " asked Luke, hoarsely.

" There was an inquest on him two days after, zir. Lor! they think nothing of shooting down a man."

The fog was now denser than ever—so thick, that from the horse's head where Luke stood the front of the fly was hardly visible. He was thinking with a chill of horror of the possibility of any such incident occurring that day, when once more there was a shout and a shot, followed by another; and, to Luke's horror, the window of the fly was let down.

" Why, what do they find to shoot here ? " said the Churchwarden, sharply ; " hares or wild deer ? "

" Men, zir," said the driver, quickly ; and as he spoke there was a loud panting noise, and a dimly-seen figure darted out of the mist at right angles to the road and dashed heavily against the horse, to fall back with a heavy groan.

CHAPTER XIV.

THE CONVICT'S ESCAPE.

THE quiet, half-asleep horse, dreamily hunting for grains of corn amidst a great deal of chaff, threw up its head and made a violent plunge forward, but was checked on the instant by the driver.

"What is it?" cried Portlock, leaping from the fly, as Sage uttered a cry.

By this time Luke was trying to lift the man, who had fallen almost at his feet, and drawing him away from the horse's hoofs, where he lay in imminent danger of being kicked.

As far as Luke could see, he was a tall, gaunt, broad-shouldered fellow, and it needed not the flyman's information for him to know that it was a convict—his closely-cropped hair and hideous gray dress told that more plainly than words could tell.

"What does it mean?" said the Church-warden again. "Some one hurt?"

As he spoke, Luke Ross, who had laid the man down, uttered an exclamation of horror. His hands were wet with blood.

"He is wounded!" said Luke, in a whisper, as he drew out his handkerchief, and sank upon one knee. "Don't let Mrs. Mallow come near."

His words of warning were too late, for just then the figure of Sage Mallow seemed to loom out of the fog, coming timidly forward with outspread hands like a person in the dark.

"He's hit hard," said the driver. "Poor chap! there's no escape for him."

"Let his head rest upon your arm," said Luke, hastily. "Mr. Portlock, tear my hand-kerchief into three strips, and give me yours. The poor fellow is bleeding horribly."

"Who's that? Where am I? Stand back, cowards! Fire, then, and be damned."

A low, wailing cry of horror checked him. and Sage Mallow flung herself upon her knees beside the injured man.

"Cyril! Husband!" she cried, wildly.

The convict started violently, and drew himself back.

"Sage!" he panted. "You—here?"

"Yes—yes!" she cried. "What is it? Are you hurt?"

"Hurt? Ha—ha—ha!"

He laughed a strange, ghastly laugh.

"I made a bolt for it. The brutes fired at me—shot me like a dog."

"Don't speak," said Luke, quickly. "Lie still, and let me try to stop this bleeding."

"Yes; stop it quick!" gasped the injured man. "Yes, that's it—in the chest—it felt red hot; but it did not stop me running, doctor. Lucky you were here."

Luke raised his face involuntarily, and the men were face to face.

"Luke Ross!" gasped Cyril; and for a few moments, as Sage and Luke knelt on either side of the wounded man, he gazed from one to the other.

"Got a divorce?" he said, with a harsh laugh. "Are you married?"

"No," cried Portlock, in a loud, emphatic voice. "Sage was coming to see you with me."

"Then—then," panted the wounded man. fiercely, "what does he do here?"

" I came at your father's wish, Cyril Mallow," said Luke. softly, for somehow his own father's words seemed to be repeating themselves in his ear. "I obtained the order."

" For my release ?" cried Cyril, wildly.

" For a visit," replied Luke. "Now, take my advice. Be silent ; exertion makes your wound bleed more."

"Curse them ! no wonder," groaned the unhappy man ; and he drew his breath with a low hiss. " God ! it's awful pain."

" Help me to lift him into the fly," whispered Luke to Portlock and the driver.

" Cyril—speak to me," whispered Sage, piteously. "You are not badly hurt ?"

"Murdered," he groaned. "Oh, if I had but a rifle and strength."

"Hush !" said Luke, sternly, "you are

wasting what you have left. Are you ready, driver?"

"There'll be no end of a row about it when the warders come, but I'll chance it, zir. Stop a moment, and I'll open the farther door. It will be easier to get him in."

"Who said warders?" panted Cyril, in excited tones. "Are they here?"

"No, no. Pray be silent," whispered Luke. "Mrs. Mallow, you must rise."

"No, no, I will not leave him," cried Sage.

"We are going to try and get him down into the town, Sage dear," said her uncle, gently; "to a doctor, girl."

She suffered her uncle to raise her up, and then the three men bent down over Cyril to bear him to the carriage.

"Stop!" he said, faintly. "I am not ready. Something—under—my head—the blood——"

Luke raised his head, and he breathed more freely, but lay with his eyes closed, the lids quivering slightly, as Sage knelt beside him once again, and wiped the clammy dew from his brow.

"It don't matter at present, gentlemen," said the driver. "I couldn't drive through this fog. We should be upset."

Just then shouts were heard close at hand, and the injured man opened his eyes and fixed them in the direction of the sound.

"Demons!" he muttered, just as there was another shot, and a loud shriek as of some one in agony.

"Another down," panted Cyril, with great effort, as he seemed to be listening intently.

"How long will it take us to get back to the town?" said Luke, quickly.

"Two hours, sir, if the fog holds up. If it goes on like this no man can say."

"Mr. Portlock," said Luke, as he motioned to Sage to take his place in supporting the wounded man's head, "what is to be done? I am no surgeon, and my bandaging is very rough. He is bleeding to death, I am sure," he whispered. "We must have a surgeon. Had I not better summon help?"

"Where from?"

"From the prison. A shout would bring the warders."

"I hear what you say," cried Cyril, fiercely. "Sage, that man is going to betray me to those blood-hounds."

"Luke!" cried Sage, who was almost mad with grief.

"There is no surgical help to be got but from the prison," said Luke, calmly. "I proposed to send for it by the warders."

"Too late," said the injured man, in a low voice. "Fifty surgeons could not save me now. Let me be."

"What shall I do?" whispered Luke.

"Poor fellow! We had better call the men."

"It would kill him," groaned Luke; and he stood hesitating, Cyril watching him the while with a sneering laugh upon his lips.

"It's a sovereign reward, lawyer," he said, faintly. "Are you going to earn it?"

For answer Luke knelt down there in the mist, and poured a few drops of spirit from his flask between the wounded man's lips.

He was about to rise, but Cyril uttered a painful sob and caught at his hand.

"I didn't mean it," he whispered. "I'm a

bad one, and the words came. I'd say God—bless you—but—no good—from me."

Luke's cold thin hand closed upon the labour-hardened palm of the wounded man, and he remained there kneeling with Sage, who held the other hand between both of hers, and gazed helplessly, and as if stunned, at her husband's face.

"Glad—you came, Sage, once more," he said. "Poor little widow!" he added, with a curious laugh.

"Had we not better get the prison doctor to you, Mallow?" said Luke.

"No good," he replied. "The game's up, man. I know. Sage—tell the old lady I thought about her—a deal. Have they found poor Ju?"

She stared at him still, for there was not one loving word to her—not one question about his children.

"Poor thing! Always petted me," he gasped—"poor mother!"

Just then there were voices heard close at hand, the trampling of feet; and Cyril Mallow's eyes seemed to dilate.

"Hallo, here!" cried a rough voice, as four men seemed to appear suddenly out of the cold gray mist. "Seen anything of—— Oh, here we are, Jem; one of the wounded birds."

The speaker, who was in the uniform of a warder, strode up, and, bending down, roughly seized Cyril by the shoulder.

"Didn't get off this time, 'Underd and seven," he said. "Nice dance you've——"

"Hands off, fellow!" cried Luke, indignantly. "Do you not see that he is badly hurt?"

"Who are you?" cried the warder, fiercely. "Don't you resist the law. Now then, 'Underd and seven, up with you. No shamming, you know."

He caught the dying man's arm, as Cyril gazed defiantly in his face, and made a snatch, as if to drag him up, when, exasperated beyond bearing at the fellow's brutality, and on seeing Sage's weak effort to shield her husband, Luke started up, and struck the ruffian so fierce a blow, full on the cheek, that he staggered back a few steps, and nearly fell.

He was up again directly, as his three

companions levelled their pieces, and the sharp click, click of the locks were heard.

"Down with him, lads!" cried the warder. "It's a planned thing. They were waiting with that fly."

The warders came on, but Luke did not shrink.

"You know," he said, firmly, "that your man exceeded his duty. Here is the Home Secretary's order for us to see this prisoner. I shall report to-day's proceedings, you may depend."

"We've got our duty to do, sir," said one of the men roughly. But he took the paper, and read it.

"Seems all right," he whispered. "Keep quiet, Smith. They couldn't get away if they wanted."

"How long would it take to fetch the surgeon?" said Luke, sternly; "or could we get him to the prison through the fog?"

"I think we could lead the horse," said the warder addressed, who began to feel some misgivings about the day's work, as he truly read Cyril Mallow's ghastly face.

"Luke—Luke Ross," said a faint voice that he did not seem to recognize, and he turned and knelt down once more by the wounded man, the warders closing in, to make sure that it was no trick.

"Ross—my hand," panted Cyril. "Fog's —getting thick—and dark. Smith—you fired —but—do you hear—I've got away."

There was a terrible pause here, and, to a man, the warders turned away, for they saw what was coming now.

"Luke Ross—good fellow—" panted the dying man—"Sage—my wife—little ones."

His eyes seemed to give the meaning to his words, as, still heedless of his wife's presence, he gazed in those of the man whose life he had seemed to blast.

"Wife—little ones. God for——"

"——give you, Cyril Mallow," whispered Luke, bending lower, "as I do, from my soul."

CHAPTER XV.

WIDOWED INDEED.

" Better take the lady away, sir," said the warder whom Luke had last addressed, and who had shown some rough feeling, as he beckoned him aside. " There'll be an inquest, of course, and I must have your card and the names of the others. There's sure to be a row, too, about your hitting Smith."

Luke took out his card-case without a word.

" Lady his wife, sir ? " said the man.

" Yes, and her uncle," replied Luke, giving the name of the hotel where they were staying. " I think we'll come on to the prison and see the governor."

" As you like, sir," said the warder; " but if I might advise, I'd say take the lady away at once, and cool down yourself before you come. You could do no good now."

"You are right, warder," said Luke, quietly, as he slipped a couple of sovereigns into the man's hand. "Send for the proper help, and—— You understand me. He was a gentleman."

"You leave it to me, sir," said the warder; "I know he was. and a high-spirited one, too. Ah, there goes the fog."

And, as if by magic, the dense cloud of gray mist rolled away, and the sun shone down brightly upon the little white cambric handkerchief wet with tears, spread a few moments before over the blindly-staring eyes looking heavenwards for the half-asked pardon.

Portlock was standing there, resting his hands upon his stout umbrella, gazing at where his niece knelt as if in prayer by her husband's corpse, and he started slightly as Luke laid a hand upon his shoulder.

"Let us go back," he whispered, and he pointed to Sage.

The old farmer went to her and took her hand.

"Sage, my child," he whispered, "come: let us go."

She looked up at him with a blank, woe-begone aspect, and clung to his hand.

"Not one loving word, uncle," she said, slowly, but in a voice that reached no other ears. "Not one word for me, or for my little orphans. Oh, Cyril, Cyril," she moaned, as she bent over him, raising the kerchief and kissing his brow, "did you love me as I loved you?"

She rose painfully as her uncle once more took her hand to lead her to the fly, where he seated himself by her side, Luke taking his place by the driver; and as they drove sadly back to the old cathedral town, the fog that had been over the land appeared to cling round and overshadow their hearts.

It seemed to Luke as he sat there thinking of Sage's sufferings that Nature was cruel, and as if she was rejoicing over Cyril Mallow's death, for the scene now looked so bright and fair. He wished that the heavens would weep, to be in unison with the unhappy woman's feelings, and that all around should wear a mourning aspect in place of looking so bright and gay. Upon his right the deep blue sea danced in the brilliant sunshine. Far behind the gray fog was scudding over the high lands, looking like a veil of silver ever changing in its hues. Here and there the glass of some conservatory flashed in the sun-rays and darted pencils of glittering light. The tints upon the hills, too, seemed brighter than when they came, and he gazed at them with a dull, chilling feeling of despair.

It seemed to him an insult to the suffering woman within the fly, and with his heart throbbing painfully in sympathy with her sorrow, he thought how strangely these matters had come about.

For the past three months this idea had been in his head : to obtain the order for Sage to see her husband ; but he had had great difficulty in obtaining that he sought, and now that he had achieved his end, what had it brought? Sorrow and despair—a horror such as must cling even to her dying day.

The driver respected his companion's silence for a time, but finding at last that there was no prospect of Luke speaking, he ventured upon a remark—

" Very horrid, zir, warn't it ?'

" Terrible, my man, terrible," said Luke, starting from his reverie.

" I shall be called at the inquest, I s'pose. This makes the third as I've been had up to, and all for convicts zhot when trying to escape. I don't think it ought to be 'lowed."

Luke was silent, and the man made no further attempts at conversation on their way to the hotel.

The inquest followed in due course, and in accordance with the previous examinations of the kind. The convict who attempted to escape did it at his own risk, his life being, so to say, forfeit to the laws, and after the stereo-typed examinations of witnesses, the regular verdict in such cases was returned, the chaplain improving his discourse on the following Sunday by an allusion to the escaped man's awful fate, and the necessity for all present bearing their punishment with patience and meekness to the end.

The warning had such a terrible effect upon

the men that not a single attempt to escape occurred afterwards for forty-eight hours, that is to say, until the next sea-fog came over the land, when three men from as many working parties darted off, and of these only one was recaptured, so that the lesson taught by Cyril Mallow's death was without effect.

There was some talk of a prosecution of Luke for striking the warder, but on the governor arriving at a knowledge of the facts, he concluded that it would be better not to attack one so learned in the law; besides which, the authorities were always glad to have anything connected with one of their judicial murders put out of sight as soon as possible, lest people of Radical instincts should make a stir in Parliament, and there should be a great call for statistics, a Committee of Inquiry, and other troublesome affairs. Consequently no more was said, and Luke Ross, after seeing Sage and her uncle to the station, returned to his solitary chambers, and laboured hard at the knotty cases that were thrust constantly into his hands.

For work was the opiate taken by Luke Ross

to ease the mental pain he so often suffered
when he allowed his thoughts to dwell upon
the past. He found in it relief, and, unconsciously, it brought him position and wealth.

He had not revisited Lawford, but from
time to time the solicitor there who had the
settlement of his father's affairs sent him
statements, accompanying them always with a
little business-like chat, that he said he thought
his eminent fellow-townsman would like to
have.

Luke used to smile at that constantly-recur-
ring term, " eminent fellow-townsman," which
the old solicitor seemed very fond of using;
but he often used to sigh as well when he read
of the changes that took place as time glided
on. How that Fullerton had ceased to carp
at church matters, and raise up strife against
church rates, being called to his fathers, and
lying very peacefully in his coffin when the
man he had so often denounced read the
solemn service of the church, and stood by as
he was laid in that churchyard.

The Rector, too, Luke learned, had grown
very old and broken of late, and it was

expected, people said, that poor Mrs. Mallow could not last much longer, for she had been smitten more sorely at the news of the death of her erring son, the paralysis having taken a greater hold, and weakened terribly her brain.

"Old Mr. Mallow goes a good deal to Kilby Farm," the solicitor said in one of his letters, "and the little grandchildren go about with him in the woods. Portlock talks of giving up his farm and retiring, but he'll never do it as long as he lives, and so I tell him.

"If there's any farther news I will save it, and send it with my next," he continued. "But I should advise you to take Warton's offer for the house in the market-place on a lease of seven (7), fourteen (14), or twenty-one (21) years, determinable on either side. He will put in a new plate-glass front, and do all repairs himself. He is a substantial man, Warton, and you could not do better with the property.—I am, dear sir, your obedient servant,

"JAMES LITTLER.

"P.S.—I have directed this letter to your chambers in King's Bench Walk. I little thought when I drew up the minutes of meeting deciding on your appointment as Master of Lawford School—an arrangement opposed, as you may remember, in meeting, by late Fullerton—I should ever have the honour of addressing you as an eminent counsel."

Luke wrote back by return :—

"Dear Mr. Littler,—Thank you for your kind management of my property. I hold Mr. Warton in the greatest respect, and there is no man in Lawford I would sooner have for my tenant. But there are certain reasons, which you may consider sentimental, against the arrangement. I wish the old house and its furniture to remain quite untouched, and widow Lane to stay there as long as she will. She was very kind to my father in his last illness, and she has had her share of trouble. I am sure he would have wished her to stay.

"Very glad to hear of any little bits of news. Yes, certainly, put my name down for what you think right for the coal fund and the other charity.—Very truly yours,

"Luke Ross."

CHAPTER XVI.

AFTER FOUR YEARS.

Four years in the life of a busy man soon glide away, and after that lapse there were certain little matters in connection with his late father's property, that Luke seized upon as an excuse for going down to Lawford once again.

He had one primary object for going, one that he had nursed now for these four years, and had dwelt upon in the intervals of his busy toil.

In spite of all bitterness of heart, he had from time to time awakened to the fact that the old love was not dead. There had always been a tiny spark hidden deeply, but waiting for a kindly breath to make it kindle into a vivid flame.

His position had led him into good society, and he had been frequently introduced to what people who enjoyed such matters termed eligible matches, but it soon became evident to all the matchmakers that the successful barrister, the next man spoken of for silk, was not a marrying man; in short, that he had no heart.

No heart!

Luke Ross knew that he had, and from time to time he would take out his old love, and think over it and wonder.

"Four years since," he said, one evening, as he sat alone in his solitary chambers. "Why not?"

Then he fell into a fit of self-examination.

"Cyril Mallow seemed to ask me to be protector to his wife and children, and I would have done anything I could, but Portlock and Cyril's father have always met Littler with the same excuse. 'There is plenty for them, and the offer would only give Mrs. Cyril pain.'"

But why not now?

He sat thinking, gazing up at the bronzed busts of great legal luminaries passed away, and at the dark shadows they cast upon the walls.

"Do I love her? Heaven knows how truly and how well."

He smiled then—a pleasant smile, which

seemed to take away the hardness from his thoughtful face.

But it was not of Sage he was thinking, but of her two little girls and his meeting with them in the Kilby lane.

"God bless them!" he said, half aloud, "I love them with all my heart."

The next day he was on his way down to Lawford, a calm, stern, middle-aged man, thinking of how the time had fled since, full of aspirations, he had come up to fight the battle for success. Sixteen years ago now, and success was won; but he was not happy. There was an empty void in his breast that he had never filled, and as he lay back in his corner of the carriage, he fell into a train of pleasanter thoughts.

The time had gone by for young and ardent love; but why should not he and Sage be happy still for the remainder of their days?

And then, in imagination, he saw them both going hand in hand down-hill, happy in the love of those two girls, whom he meant it to be his end and aim to win more and more to himself.

"God bless them!" he said again, as he

thought of the flowers the younger one had offered him, of the kiss the other had imprinted upon his hand; and at last, happier and brighter than he had felt for years, he leaped out of the carriage and ordered a fly and pair to take him to Kilby Farm.

His joyous feelings seemed even on the increase as he neared the place, in spite of the tedious rate at which they moved, and turning at last after the long ride into the Kilby lane, he came in sight of the snug old farm just as the setting sun was gilding the windows.

The Churchwarden was at the door with a smile of welcome as Luke leaped from the fly and warmly grasped his hand.

"I knew you would come," he said; "but how quick you have been. When did you get my letter?"

"Your letter?"

"Yes; asking you to come. She begged me to write."

"Then it was inspiration that brought me here. She will welcome me as I wish," he cried. "I have not had your letter. Take me to her at once, I have wasted too much time as it is."

"Heaven bless you for coming, Luke," said the old man, with trembling voice. "It was the mistake of my life that I did not let you wed."

"Never too late to mend," said Luke, smiling, and then he saw something in the farmer's face that turned him ghastly white.

"Sage?" he gasped. "Is she ill?"

"Ill?" faltered the farmer. "I forgot you could not know. Luke, my boy! my poor bairn! She cannot last the night."

"Stop that fly," panted Luke. "A telegram—to London—to Sir Roland Murray—I know his address—to come at once, at any cost. Paper, man, for God's sake—quick—pens—ink. Moments mean life."

"Moments mean death, Luke Ross," said the Churchwarden, solemnly. "My boy, I have not spared my useless money. It could not save her life. She knows that you have come. She heard the wheels."

Luke followed the old man to the upper chamber, fragrant with sweet country scents, and then staggered to the bedside, to throw himself upon his knees.

"Sage! My love!" he panted, as he caught her hand. "You must live to bless me—my love, whom I have loved so long. It is not too late—it is not too——"

He paused as he too truly read the truth, and bent down to catch her fleeting breath that strove to shape itself in words.

"I could not die until I saw you once again. No; Luke — friend — brother — it could not have been. Quick," she cried. "My children —quick!"

The Churchwarden went softly from the room, while poor old Mrs. Portlock sank down in a chair by the window, and covered her face with her hands.

"I have been dying these two years, Luke," whispered Sage, faintly. "Now, tell me that you forgive the past."

"Forgive? It has been forgiven these many years," he groaned. "But, Sage, speak to me, my own old love."

She smiled softly in his face.

"No," she said, "not your love, Luke. My children. You will—for my sake—Luke?"

He could not speak, but clasped the little

ones to his breast—partly in token of his silent vow—partly that they might not see Sage Mallow's sun set, as the great golden orb sank in the west.

Death had his work to do at Lawford as elsewhere, and the sleepy little town was always waking up to the fact that some indweller had passed away.

It was about a week earlier that Polly Morrison sat waiting and working by her one candle, which shed its light upon her pleasant, comely face. The haggard, troubled look had gone, and though there were lines in her forehead, they seemed less the lines of care than those of middle age.

Every now and then she looked up and listened for the coming step, but there was only an occasional sough of the wind, and the hurried rush of the waters over the ford, for the stream was high, and the swirling pools beneath the rugged old willow pollards deep.

Polly heard the rush of the waters, and a shudder passed through her, for she recalled Jock Morrison's threat about Cyril years ago.

This set her thinking of him and his end; from that she journeyed on in thought to Sage Mallow, the pale, careworn widow, slowly sinking into her grave; and this suggestive theme made the little matronly-looking body drop her work into her lap, and sit gazing at the glowing wood fire, wondering whether Mrs. Mallow or Sage would die first, and whether Miss Cynthia, as she always called her, was soon coming down to Gatley so as to be near.

Then her thoughts in spite of herself went back to another death scene, and the tears gathered in her eyes as she saw once more that early Sunday morning, when the earth lay dark in a little mound beneath the willow, where a religiously-tended little plot of flowers always grew.

"I wish Tom would come back," she said, plaintively. "It is so lonely when he has to go into town."

She made an effort to resume her work, and stitched away busily for a time, but her nimble fingers soon grew slow, and dropped once more into her lap, as the waters roared loudly once again, and she thought of Cyril Mallow, then of Jock, lastly of Julia.

"I wonder where they are?" she said, softly. "Sometimes I've thought it might be my fault, though I don't see how— At last!"

There was a step outside and with brightening face she snuffed the candle, and glanced at the table to see that Tom's supper was as he liked it to be.

Then she stopped in alarm, gazing sharply at the door, for it was not Tom's step, but a faintly heard hesitating pace, half drowned by the rushing noise from the ford.

"Who can it be?" she muttered, and then her face turned ghastly white.

"Something has happened to Tom!"

She stood there as if paralyzed, as a faint tapping sounded on the door—the soft hesitating tap of some one's fingers; and the summons set Polly trembling with dread.

"What can it be?" she faltered. "Oh, for shame! what a coward I am!" she cried, as she roused herself, and going to the door, her hand was on the latch just as the summons was faintly repeated.

"Who's there? What is it?" cried Polly, stoutly; but there was no answer, and taking up the candle, she held it above her head and flung open the door, to see a thin, ill-clad woman holding on by one of the rough fir poles that formed the porch, gazing at her with wild, staring eyes, her face cadaverous, thin, and pinched, and her pale lips parted as if to speak.

"Miss Julia!" cried Polly, with a faint shriek, and setting down the candle, she caught the tottering figure by the arm and drew her in, the door swung to, and the wanderer was held tightly to her breast.

"Oh, my dear, my dear!" sobbed Polly. "How could you—how could you? Oh, that it should come to this!"

Her visitor did not answer, but seemed to yield herself to the affectionate caresses that were showered upon her, a faint smile dawning upon her thin lips, and her eyes half closing as from utter weariness and pain.

"Why you're wet. and like ice!" cried Polly, as she realized the facts. "Oh, my poor dear! How thin! How ill you look! Oh, my dear, my dear!"

She burst into a piteous fit of sobbing, but her hands were busy all the time, as she half led, half carried her visitor to Tom's big Windsor chair, and then piled up some of the odd blocks of wood, of which there were always an abundance from the shop.

"Oh, what shall I do?" muttered Polly; and then her ideas took the customary womanly route for the panacea for all ills, a cup of tea, which was soon made, and a few mouthfuls seemed to revive the fainting woman.

"She ought to have the doctor," muttered Polly. "Oh, if Tom would only come!" Then aloud—"Oh, Miss Julia, my dear, my dear!"

"Hush!" said her visitor, in a low, painful voice, as if repeating words that she had learned by heart; "the Julia you knew is dead."

"Oh, no, no, my dear young mistress," sobbed Polly, and she went down upon her knees, and threw her arms round the thin, cold figure in its squalid clothes. "Tom will be home directly, and he shall fetch the doctor and master. Oh, my dear, my dear! that it should come to this! But tell me, have you left Jock Morrison?"

The wretched woman shuddered.

"They have taken him away," she whispered; "he was in trouble—with some keepers—but he will be out some day, and I must go to him again. He will want me, Polly—and I must go!"

Polly Morrison gazed at her with horror, hardly recognizing a lineament of the girl in whose soft hair she had taken such pride, and whom she had admired in her youth and beauty.

"But you must not go back," cried the little woman. "There, there, let your head rest back on the chair. Let me go and fetch you a pillow."

"No, don't go, Polly," and the thin hands closed tightly about those so full of ministering care. "I'm tired—I've walked so far."

"Walked? Miss Julia!"

"Hush! Julia is dead," she moaned. "Yes, walked. It was in—Hampshire, I think— weeks ago."

And you walked? Oh, my dear, my dear!" sobbed Polly.

"I was—so weary—so tired, Polly," moaned the wretched woman; "and—I was—always thinking—of your garden—that little baby—so sweet—so sweet."

"Oh, Miss Julia, Miss Julia, pray, pray don't!" sobbed Polly.

"Mine died—years ago—died too—they took it—took it away. I thought if I could get—get as far—you would——"

She stopped speaking, and raised herself in the chair, holding tightly by Polly Morrison's hands, and gazing wildly round the room.

"Miss Julia!"

"Is it dreaming?" she cried, in a hoarse loud voice. "No, no," she said softly, and the slow, weary, hesitating syllables dropped faintly again from her thin, pale lips. "I— tried—so hard—I want to—to see—that little little grave—Polly—the little one—asleep."

"Miss Julia! Oh, my dear, my dear."

"For—I'm—I'm tired, dear. Let—let me —see it, Polly—let me go—to sleep."

"Miss Julia—Miss Julia! Help! Tom—Tom! Quick—help! Oh! my God!"

As wild and passionate a cry as ever rose to heaven for help, but it was not answered.

And the Rev. Lawrence Paulby stood amidst the crowd that thronged Lawford churchyard,—a hushed, bare-headed crowd,—but his voice became inaudible as he tried to repeat the last words of the service beside poor Julia's grave.

THE END.